SO-EIC-543

THE
NIGHT SPIDER
CASE

THE
NIGHT SPIDER
CASE

BETTY BAKER

Macmillan Publishing Company
New York
Collier Macmillan Publishers
London

Macmillan Publishing Company
866 Third Avenue, New York, N.Y. 10022
Collier Macmillan Canada, Inc.

Printed in the United States of America
Designed by Ben Birnbaum

10 9 8 7 6 5 4 3 2 1

LIBRARY OF CONGRESS CATALOGING IN PUBLICATION DATA

Baker, Betty.

The night spider case.

SUMMARY: In the 1890's in New York City, eleven-year-
old Lambert Grew reluctantly teams up with his neighbor
Frances Ward to investigate the mystery of the empty
house next door.

[1. Mystery and detective stories. 2. New York (City)
—Fiction] I. Title
PZ7.B1693Ni 1984 [Fic] 83-22181
ISBN 0-02-708170-2

THE
NIGHT SPIDER
CASE

CHAPTER
ONE

"Good m-o-o-o-orning, La-a-ambie!"

Lambert nearly fell down the last two steps. Then he realized it couldn't be Biff Finnegan and his gang. Even when Biff used a sissy voice to sneer at Lambert, he didn't sound anything like a girl. Lambert braced himself on the broom and peeked under his bent arm.

Frances Ward stood on the sidewalk, grinning up at him. She held a large basket in front of her, both hands on the handle. Lambert straightened and scowled down at her.

"What are you doing out this early?" he said.

The sun hadn't touched even the tallest trees in Washington Square park across the street. The milkman's cart was just two short blocks away and the iceman had already delivered. But nobody else in New York was out this early. Not even the street sweepers with their white barrels on wheels. It was so quiet that Lambert could hear the iron wheels of the market carts hitting the cobblestones over on Sixth Avenue.

3

Frances bounced the basket with her knee and stared up at him, her head tilted to one side. Lambert felt like a rabbit or fat pigeon hung in the meat stall in Jefferson Market. He looked up and down the street.

There was only Mr. Schiller and his milk cart. And Frances Ward. He scowled at her again.

There was no way she could have seen him from her uncle's house, around the corner on Fifth Avenue. But if she hadn't hightailed it over here to torment him about doing the sweeping, what did she want?

Maybe it was force of habit. Frances and the girl next door had been close as fleas. Beth Ann and her family had moved to a new house at the edge of the city, way up past One Hundred Twenty-fifth Street. But maybe Frances had forgotten.

Mr. Quince had been gone nearly a month and Lambert still caught himself stopping to knock at his door on the way down to breakfast. The house next door hadn't been empty a week. And Frances had played there with Beth Ann almost every day for a couple of years, ever since her parents had been killed in a carriage crash and she'd had to move in with her uncle.

Maybe this morning she'd hopped out of bed, gotten dressed and trotted around the corner just out of habit. It wasn't an hour for visiting, but for all Lambert knew, the girls could have rolled hoops or something every day at sunrise. He sure hadn't been up to see.

"I'm collecting spiderwebs," Frances told him. She was still grinning.

Lambert jabbed the broom in the corner of the marble

4

steps. Just because he was short and skinny, it didn't mean he was weak in the head!

"What are *you*?"

"What am I what?" Lambert kept his eyes on the step he was sweeping and tried to bark his words the way Miss Beeman said the lawyer she worked for barked at her. It upset Miss Beeman just to imitate him but it didn't faze Frances any.

"What are *you* doing out this early?" she said again. When he didn't answer, she added, "I never saw anyone do the sweeping until after the milk's delivered."

That was because the maid who took out the jugs and pails was usually the third girl, the same one who did the sweeping. The one Mama had had to let go. Until they could afford to hire her back, Lambert had to do the sweeping. And he had to finish before the neighbors' maids came out and saw him.

Not that it made much difference. They could see him through a window. So could any of the neighbors who hadn't already left for the summer. The maids would gossip among themselves (they probably already knew the third girl was gone and why), but the neighbors would pretend nothing had changed so as not to embarrass Lambert's mother. The way they pretended she didn't take in boarders.

They were wealthy boarders from the sort of families Lambert's mother and father had entertained before his father died. But they were boarders all the same. Neighbors and friends called them "guests" when they had to admit they were there.

5

Grown-ups did that sometimes, just decided that something didn't count if nobody paid it any attention in public. Like Mrs. Astor's wig or Frances's uncle's getting caught in a gambling raid.

The police had been raiding and reraiding gambling dens all winter. Ladies visiting his mother and Mrs. Van Horne on Friday afternoons had talked about the newspaper accounts, shocked at so much wickedness and saying it was time the police cleaned up the city. Then the police finally raided one of the posh gambling casinos up on Fifth Avenue.

The story had covered the front pages with the famous names listed. All but Mr. Ward's were from the theater. That Friday, the ladies had talked as if they'd never seen a newspaper.

Of course, Lambert had only heard the ones who'd called after he got home from school, but he was sure none of the others had mentioned it, either. It was another of those things grown-ups all decided hadn't happened.

Lambert didn't understand it or see why they bothered. It meant he had to get up at dawn now. But he didn't like his mother to feel embarrassed, and besides, he was as anxious as his mother to get the sweeping done early.

He'd never seen Biff Finnegan in this neighborhood, but there was always a first time for everything. Look at Frances Ward nosing around before dawn. No wonder the people next door had moved.

He swept the broom as hard as he could, but the steps and sidewalks were swept every morning. He couldn't raise enough dust to chase her away. Her black cotton stockings and shiny high-buttoned shoes were soon as dusty as Lambert's, but she didn't seem to care. She probably didn't have to.

Lambert ran out of steps and she was still there, a year younger and just as tall. *Taller.* At least it seemed that way when Lambert stood on the sidewalk, too. He bent over his sweeping, trying to measure their shadows as she followed him back and forth. But she kept moving around, showing him the stuff in her basket and explaining how to spray the paint through the bent tubes. She really was collecting spiderwebs, and they had to be collected before the sun woke the bugs.

"You won't find any here," Lambert told her. "Why don't you collect in your backyard?"

Her uncle had a real garden behind his Fifth Avenue house, with brick walks and white statues and a fountain. Lambert could see it in winter from one of his bedroom windows.

"There must be a zillion spiders there," said Lambert.

"The gardener won't let me." Frances nodded at the park across the street. "I thought I'd try over there."

"You better hurry. The sun's almost up."

Lambert carried the broom up the steps and leaned it against one of the marble benches built into each end of the stoop. He grabbed the cloth he'd left there and ran back down, dusting the railing as he went.

Frances was still at the bottom, bumping the basket and watching him. "I thought you'd like to go along."

7

"I'm busy." Lambert crossed to the other railing, keeping to the bottom step. Frances went along, on the sidewalk.

"I thought the maid could do this," she said.

Lambert flushed. That was as good as saying he was doing girl's work. She was as bad as Biff Finnegan. She'd probably push him around, too; she was bigger than he was now. He wished he were safe inside, up in his room reading the rest of . ... He suddenly knew how to get rid of Frances. It would keep her from blabbing about him doing girl's work, too.

He bent over the railing and pretended to rub a spot on the brass. Without raising his head, he looked up, then down the street. Nosy Frances looked, too. Lambert bit the side of his lip to keep from laughing.

Then he said, almost in a whisper, "The maid can't do the sweeping. I need it to cover my detecting."

"What?"

Was she deaf? "I said, the maid .... "

Frances interrupted. "What are you detecting?"

"Felonies and malefactions." He spoke the words slowly. He'd read them last night and enjoyed their foursquare sound. He repeated them in a whisper, racing to reach the stoop before he finished.

He grinned, pleased with himself, and traded the cloth for a feather duster. When he turned, Frances was settling herself on the other bench.

CHAPTER
TWO

Will you go away?" Lambert whispered as loudly as he could. "You'll ruin my cover!"

"I'll help it. You really should be dressed as a maid."

Lambert gave her a dirty look. Frances held the basket on her lap and swung her feet.

"What did you detect so far?" she said.

Lambert dusted the door slowly and thought fast. Two men with canvas tool bags had gone into the empty house next door. They'd used the basement entrance under the steps that led to the wide front door. Like Lambert's house, the one on the corner was old and had been built with kitchen and dining room in the half-basement. Frances would know the men were only turning off the gas. So Lambert told her about the two he'd noticed across the street.

"One with a mustache, a derby and a cigar; the other in a work cap and carrying a measuring rod." It wasn't anything like the descriptions of felons that Pinkerton detectives wrote, but Frances wouldn't have read the stories in the *Police Gazette*. (Neither would Lambert if his mother knew.) Proud that he'd remembered as much as he had, Lambert added, "They're measuring the park."

"The city's probably going to fence it," said Frances.

Lambert, hunkered down to dust the bottom panels, turned to look at her. "They're not measuring the outside. They started where the path does and measured in."

Frances looked doubtful.

"The man in the derby has a map," Lambert added.

"How do you know?"

"It was this big." Lambert spread his hands to show her. The feather duster hit the door. "And he kept looking at it and then pointing things out to the fellow with the measuring rod. It's a map, all right." He'd convinced himself, and Frances, too, from the way she looked across the street to the park.

"Did they have a shovel?" she said.

A milk can rattled three houses down. Lambert dove for the cloth and started rubbing the brass doorknob.

Frances said, "You're lucky I came around, Lambie. Now you can go see what they're up to. Helping me collect spiderwebs is a dandy cover."

Not if Biff Finnegan saw them. With Frances there, he'd just grin at Lambert. But the grin wouldn't be friendly and the next time Biff cornered Lambert, the jeering and shoving would be worse than ever. He might even tell Lambert to put up his dukes and then blacken his eye and bloody his nose the way he had the first time. Lambert couldn't decide which would be worse: the bully catching him spraying spiderwebs with a girl or Frances finding out there was nothing to detect.

He attacked the door knocker, rubbing furiously, but all he could come up with was, "Girls aren't detectives."

"What about Loveday Brooke, Lady Detective? The *Press* ran a story about her every Thursday last winter."

"That's a made-up detective, like Sherlock Holmes. Real detectives like the Pinkertons aren't girls."

"How do you know?"

"I read about them all the time."

"Where?"

"Up in my room." Because he hid the *Police Gazette*s under his mattress.

Slowly, as if he weren't quite bright, Frances said, "In what magazine or newspaper do you read about them, Lambie?"

Lambert glared at her, too furious to think. His mother saved him.

She opened the front door and said cheerfully, "Oh, it's you, Lambert. I heard knocking and thought we had a visitor."

Lambert hadn't banged the knocker that hard. His mother must have seen Frances from the parlor window and been worrying that she'd tell her uncle about poor Mrs. Grew who couldn't afford a third maid anymore. He suspected she'd been standing behind the door, waiting for some plan to come to mind.

11

He was sure of it when his mother leaned around the doorway and said good morning to Frances.

"Good morning, Mrs. Grew." Frances was on her feet but she wasn't leaving. Just showing her manners.

"You're Mr. Ward's niece, aren't you?" said Mrs. Grew. "Frances, I believe."

"Yes, ma'am."

"Were you planning a picnic breakfast? Why don't you save that for luncheon and have breakfast with us?"

"No!" said Lambert. They had to get rid of Frances, not keep her around half the morning. He told his mother, "Frances is in a terrible hurry, Mama. She's collecting spiderwebs and it's almost too late now to find perfect ones."

But Frances squinted at the trees across the street and said, "I can still find some for the next hour or so if Lambert helps." She smiled brightly past him at his mother.

"Why, that's perfect!" said Mrs. Grew. "It'll be an hour until breakfast is served."

Lambert wondered if Frances had known. He decided she had. Almost everyone in the neighborhood had their breakfast rolls delivered from the Vienna Bakery. Frances wasn't just nosy; she was sneaky, too.

She said, "Thank you, Mrs. Grew. I'll be delighted to breakfast with you."

Now Lambert wouldn't get back to his *Police Gazette* for hours. He wished Frances would go look for spiders in Madison Square park or that big new Central Park at the end of the city. She could get lost in that one.

Mrs. Grew said, "You may leave your basket in the kitchen, Frances."

"No, thank you."

Lambert's mother looked confused and flustered. Lambert guessed she'd wanted Frances to go downstairs and see Bridget and Molly helping the cook. Then, when Bridget changed her apron and put on a cap to serve breakfast, Frances would think she was a third maid. And if she thought the two she'd seen downstairs were just kitchen help, she might believe Mama had as big a staff as her uncle. Only Frances didn't have a picnic in her basket so it hadn't worked. Nothing seemed to work with Frances.

Mrs. Grew smiled bravely and said, "Well, don't spoil your appetites. Our cook . . . . "

The milk cart banged and rattled to a stop next door. Mrs. Grew turned to look, saw the broom and feather duster on the other bench and frowned.

"Lambert, what are those doing here?" she said, just as if she hadn't sent him out with them.

And just as if he'd really been detecting, Lambert said, "I needed them for something."

He liked it. It was as if they were two Pinkertons protecting each other from a dangerous malefactor. His mother even gave him a chance to escape and a message to deliver to the office.

"Take them down where they belong," she told him. "And tell Mrs. Magee there will be another guest for breakfast."

"Yes, ma'am." Lambert dragged the broom down the

marble steps, then around and down the shorter flight of plain ones to the basement entry. He didn't have to pretend being mad. Only it was sneaky Frances he was mad at, not his mother.

He left the broom, duster and cloth in a big room half-filled with trunks and crates. It had been the dining room before dumbwaiters were invented and food could be sent upstairs. Now it was used for storage. The crates and most of the trunks belonged to Mrs. Van Horne, things she'd kept after she'd sold her enormous house. The bicycle was Mr. Carter's.

It was a crack wheel, a top-of-the-line Columbia too big for Lambert to ride and too expensive for him to hope for, especially with most of the second floor empty. He flicked the duster over the bicycle before he went in the kitchen.

Bridget was slicing ham. Mrs. Magee sat at the table, going over menus and making lists on smoothed bits of butcher's wrap. Lambert gave her the message.

"Man or woman?" she wanted to know. It would make a difference in how much she needed to cook.

"The suite or the room?" asked Bridget. "If it's the suite, maybe we'll have Elsie back."

Lambert had to tell them that neither had been rented. They weren't likely to be, either, until fall. The sort of people who recommended Mama's guests were in Saratoga or Bar Harbor or the mountains of Virginia for the summer.

Other summers it hadn't mattered. Mr. Quince had lived in the second-floor suite almost as long as Mrs. Van Horne had been in the one below. And it was Mrs. Van

14

Horne who'd talked Mama into taking paying guests after Lambert's father died.

"It's better than being a poor relation in Schenectady," Lambert remembered her telling Mama. Lambert, who'd met his cousins and aunt from Schenectady, had silently agreed.

Mrs. Van Horne was more of an aunt than Lambert's real one. She'd grown up with his grandmother and known his mother all her life. Which was probably why she'd pushed Mrs. Grew into taking paying guests, though she claimed it was purely selfish.

"I needed a place to live graciously," she said, "and not have to waste my time and energy taking care of that white elephant."

Her house had been even larger than Frances's uncle's. Lambert remembered halls full of scurrying servants and talk of balls and dinners for sixty. Considering how busy Mrs. Van Horne was now, Lambert didn't doubt she'd wanted to be free of the house. But she'd been a widow for years, and Lambert didn't think she'd have bothered moving if his mother hadn't needed help.

He suspected Mrs. Van Horne had paid for the remodeling, too. One of the two arguments he knew about had been when Mrs. Van Horne insisted the workmen put another bath above the one being built between the two rooms that made up her suite.

She'd told Lambert's mother, "You cannot expect four of your guests to share one bathroom, Mabel. They'd have to run on schedule, like trains. Besides, you'll get more for the suite than the other two rooms combined."

Which proved to be true after Mrs. Van Horne won the second argument, too, the one about the rates. The ones she suggested had shocked Lambert's mother.

"Nonsense," Mrs. Van Horne had told her. "There are always sons of fine families needing a home between university and marriage. They can afford to pay well and won't appreciate it if they don't. And don't worry, Mabel." The corners of Mrs. Van Horne's mouth twitched. "It will be perfectly respectable with me here to chaperone."

That last had made Lambert anxious for a couple of years. He'd compared each new guest to his memory of his father and worried that his mother might not see them the same way.

But she seemed content with her life as a businesswoman, though she'd be the last to admit that's what she was. They could no longer afford to keep a carriage but life went on much the same. Mrs. Grew received the courtesies and invitations Mr. Grew's widow should receive and Lambert went to the proper schools. They might even have managed a bicycle if Mr. Quince hadn't retired and moved to Florida and the young man in the rear room hadn't sneaked out owing two months' rent. And both in the spring.

It wouldn't have worried Lambert (except for getting caught sweeping) if he hadn't finished at his old school. The one he was enrolled in for September meant crossing Biff Finnegan's territory twice a day. If he didn't get a bicycle . . . .

Mrs. Magee was asking him something. She repeated it. "Who is it, then, Lambert? For breakfast."

16

"Oh. It's Frances Ward."

The cook frowned at him, thinking Frances was his fault. Mrs. Magee didn't like her meals upset by unexpected guests.

"Mama invited her."

"She better not want an omelet."

Molly ran in for the milk jugs. Lambert looked wistfully at the ham. He'd been up so early, his stomach thought it was noon. But he didn't dare snitch any, not with Bridget disappointed and Mrs. Magee mad.

He followed Molly out. Frances was waiting.

She leaned over the railing to tell him, "Hurry up, Lambie. You're letting them get away." Then she spun around and called, "Good morning!" to Mr. Schiller and darted in front of the milk cart.

Mr. Schiller had to rein old Rosie in short. He glared at Lambert as if it were his fault. Lambert hoped Frances stepped in a big pile of horse droppings.

If she did, she didn't stop to clean it off. When Lambert finally got around the milk cart, Frances was past the arch and into the park. She waited for him where one of the cross paths met the paths that ran like spokes from the sides and corners of the park to the fountain at the center.

"We'll cover more ground if we split up," she said. "You go that way and I'll go this."

It was the only good suggestion she'd made. Lambert hurried down the cross path until he looked back and found Frances was out of sight. Then he stuck his hands in the pockets of his knickers and strolled between the rows of empty benches.

He couldn't go home. His mother was expecting Frances for breakfast. She'd want to know why she wasn't with him. If he said Frances was sick or had changed her mind, Mama would think Frances and her uncle no longer considered the Grews socially acceptable. If he said Frances had gotten mad and gone home, Mama would send him to apologize and then telephone to make sure he'd done it properly.

He'd say Frances was too busy collecting spiderwebs to eat breakfast. It would serve Frances right. Lambert grinned. But Mama would want to know why he'd left her. He could think of lots of good reasons, including the truth, but his mother wouldn't understand any of them. A gentleman never abandoned a lady. Lambert sighed and strolled on.

He saw two spiderwebs on bushes but no sign of anyone measuring or digging. Lambert couldn't decide if that would discourage Frances.

Sun shone through the trees now. A big patch of sunshine showed where Lambert's path met one leading to the center. He was almost to it when he heard voices. One of them was Biff Finnegan's.

The boys were on the other path, headed for the fountain. They couldn't see Lambert for the bushes, but the bushes gave out long before the crossing.

Lambert glanced back. The only things within reach big enough to hide him were the benches. But they were made of narrow green slats with spaces between. The closest one, though, had a young sycamore behind it.

Bridget always said that folks mostly never looked up

18

and Lambert figured she knew. When she hurried the dusting, she skipped the picture rails and the wide carved moldings over the doors and Mama hadn't caught her yet.

Lambert jumped on the bench, stood on the back and hauled himself onto the nearest branch. He lay gripping the branch with arms and legs, hoping Biff wouldn't notice it was swaying, and stared down at a cap just like his lying on the bench.

CHAPTER
THREE

He loosened a hand and felt his head. The cap was his, all right. But it didn't have his name on it. It could have been lost by anyone. Maybe Biff wouldn't think to look up when he found it. If he did, Lambert would climb higher. Biff was too much heavier to reach him. Lambert could just stay in the tree until there were people around. If he didn't starve and fall first.

Where was nosy Frances when she could help?

He heard footsteps: more than one set. When he hung his head down beside the branch, he got a clear view of the crossing. Biff and the two biggest members of his gang crossed the patch of sunshine. They had their heads together and didn't even glance toward the bench and cap.

Lambert climbed up and around until he found a gap in the leaves that let him look toward the center of the park. One of the two men he'd told Frances about was standing with one foot on a bench. The map was spread on his thigh. One hand steadied the edge; the other held a half-smoked cigar. Just when Lambert was getting restless, the man looked in his direction and used the thumb of his cigar hand to push back his derby. Biff and his pals walked up to him.

"What are you doing up there, Lambie?"

Lambert whispered a cuss word. Nosy Frances stood on the path holding her basket in front of her just the way she had before. She was studying Lambert the same way, too. Maybe that's why the first answer to pop into his head was, "Looking for your pernicious spiders, that's what."

She grinned. "Find any?"

"Do you think I'd be up here if I hadn't?"

"I hope it's a *Magora gibberosa*. I've been looking all morning for a *Magora gibberosa*."

If that was some kind of a trap, she wasn't going to catch Lambert Grew. "I don't know what spider made it," he told her, "but it hasn't caught any bugs yet." And that for sure was the truth.

"You need the stuff in the basket," she said.

She couldn't climb the tree with the basket. While Lambert waited for her to find out, he watched Biff conferring with the map man.

His stomach growled. He wondered if the sycamore's green, stickery seed balls were poison. The cluster in front of him trembled and swayed. So did the branch he was sitting on.

"Hey!" He grabbed the tree trunk.

Frances climbed up beside him. She hadn't tried to bring the basket. She'd bundled stuff in a big linen napkin

21

and held the knot between her teeth. She must have folded the black paper and put it inside Lambert's cap, which now covered her hair bow.

She took a long time finding a branch that shared his view, so he had an answer ready when she took the bundle out of her mouth and asked where the web was.

"With all the shaking you did, I put my foot through it."

"I thought you might." She undid the knot and spread the cloth on her lap. It wasn't a napkin, Lambert saw, but one of her uncle's fine linen handkerchiefs. And it held wedge-shaped scones. She handed him one. "They're yesterday's, but it was all I could find."

The scone was hard and crumbly but she'd jellied as well as buttered it. Lambert thanked her and meant it.

"You're welcome. Is that one of the men you're detecting?" Frances jabbed her scone at the group beside the bench. The tip of the scone fell into her lap and rolled off. Frances was too interested in the map man to notice. "Is he?"

Lambert's mouth was full of hard crumbs. He nodded.

So did Frances. "I thought so, soon as I saw them. The one with the measuring stick's over there." She pointed the scone and lost another chunk.

If she didn't want it, Lambert wished she'd offer it to him while there was still some left.

"You were right, Lambie. It's a map. I asked him for directions and saw it."

He'd have been more pleased at being right if she hadn't called him Lambie. If she did it again, he'd just take that scone away from her. He finished his, licked his fingers and watched the map man and Biff.

The man was doing the talking, giving instructions or offering a deal. Whichever it was, Biff agreed after glancing at his friends. The man took his map farther into the park. The boys came back the way they'd gone.

They were excited now, their voices louder. As they passed, Biff was saying, "... dig up the rest easy. Pure gravy, that's what . . . ."

"Lambie!"

He watched the scone break a twig and disappear through the leaves. She'd dropped it just to grab the arm he had wrapped around the tree trunk.

"It's a *treasure* map, Lambie!"

"You're touched in the head. Nobody holds a treasure map up where anybody passing by can see it."

"I didn't pass by. I walked right up and looked."

"And I suppose there were sixteen footprints going north by northwest from the old pump?"

She went from angry to interested. "What pump?"

"The one people got their water from before they built the reservoir up at Fortieth Street."

She looked as if she didn't believe him.

"It's true. Mrs. Van Horne told me. There were pumps all over the city." Lambert brightened. If food wouldn't get Frances to breakfast, maybe Mrs. Van Horne would. He added, "She knows all kinds of stories about the old days. If anybody was burying treasure, she'd know about it."

23

Frances studied him a second, then turned and climbed down so fast she tore the knee out of her stocking. Lambert followed more carefully. He looked for the half scone when he got down but didn't see it. He didn't get his cap back, either.

"Let me wear it to the arch," Frances said, "and you don't have to carry my basket."

He had to carry it anyway, in case his mother was watching for them. He stomped along, fuming at the unfairness, while Frances chattered about buried treasure.

She wouldn't listen to reason. Lambert told her about dinner last night when Mr. Carter had said he'd dig up an old issue of the *Wheel* for Miss Beeman.

"People say it all the time," Lambert said. "They don't mean they're going to dig with a shovel."

"They do when the man who hires them has a treasure map."

Lambert agreed that the map man had probably hired Biff and his friends to do something, but it wasn't digging for treasure in Washington Square park. He said slowly and firmly, "There . . . is . . . no . . . treasure."

Frances stopped and turned to face him. "Want to bet?"

He'd managed to save eight dollars and forty-three cents toward a bicycle. He didn't want to risk a penny of it, but if he didn't take the bet, Frances would win.

She said, "If there's a treasure, you have to help me find it. If there isn't, then I'll help you detect." She held out her hand. "Deal?"

"Deal," said Lambert, and shook her hand. He couldn't

help grinning. There wasn't any treasure and he sure wasn't doing any detecting.

"Race you to the door!" said Frances, and took off down the path.

With a side dip, Lambert set the basket down and raced after her. As she passed the arch, the cap flew off and sailed toward him. He jumped it and kept going.

Frances had sneaked a head start, but Lambert had been running from Biff Finnegan for almost a year. He passed her on the steps and managed to get the door open for her, just as a gentleman should.

Frances gave him a furious look. Lambert grinned and went back for his cap and the basket. She hadn't expected him to drop the basket and if she'd thought he'd stop for the cap, she'd found out she was wrong.

It wasn't until he was upstairs washing for breakfast and thinking about the bet that he realized what Frances had done. Win or lose, he was going to be stuck with Frances Ward. Maybe for weeks! Had she started the race so he wouldn't have time to figure that out?

Not that it made any difference. Not even Mr. Pinkerton could find treasure or anything else to detect around here.

CHAPTER
FOUR

When Lambert got to the dining room, everyone except Mr. Carter was there. A chair for Frances had been set next to Lambert's. He settled between her and Miss Beeman.

Ordinarily, Miss Beeman couldn't afford to be one of Mama's paying guests. She was only a stenographer and typist. But she worked for Mrs. Van Horne's lawyer, and Mrs. Van Horne had discovered that she often was kept working so late that she missed her connections on the horsecars.

"Not only is that skinflint getting extra hours of work," Mrs. Van Horne had told Lambert's mother, "but the poor girl must walk a mile alone late at night. If you could find a room for her here, Mabel, she'd be just around the corner. And maybe we could put a little steel in her spine."

Mrs. Grew's worry was that Miss Beeman might already have too much steel in her spine. To Lambert's mother, working women meant "new women." And "new women" meant suffragettes who spent their nights in illegal gambling casinos and their days carrying banners around Columbia University, protesting three young women's not being allowed to enter the law school.

"It's for their own good," the president had said, "to protect them from the embarrassment of having to move in a man's world." Lambert's mother agreed, even though Mrs. Van Horne had backed the three would-be lawyers. Mrs. Grew believed a woman's place was in the home.

But she didn't have enough steel in her spine to stand up to Mrs. Van Horne. She accepted her invitation to Sunday tea. So did Miss Beeman.

Luckily, it was a warm day and the windows were open. When Lambert sat on his favorite stoop bench, he could hear everything in Mrs. Van Horne's sitting room. Miss Beeman sounded as nice as she was pretty.

Lambert's mother seemed to think so, too. After Miss Beeman left, she told Mrs. Van Horne it was a pity there wasn't a room vacant.

"If there was," Mrs. Van Horne said, "she couldn't afford it. I was thinking about that extra room up on the top floor."

"With the help?" Lambert's mother couldn't have sounded more shocked if Miss Beeman had chewed gum and dunked her tea cakes.

"But she can afford what you'd charge for that room." Mrs. Van Horne had sounded as if she was smiling.

Then they'd taken the tea things to the dumbwaiter and Lambert had missed the rest. But a week later Miss

Beeman had moved into a room across from Lambert's on the third floor, the floor his mother had reserved for the two of them.

Lambert didn't mind. He liked Miss Beeman and tried to think of things to do for her. So did his mother. Although the rule was "miss dinner, go without," when Miss Beeman had to work late, she always found a tray waiting for her in Mrs. Van Horne's parlor or, if Mrs. Van Horne had gone out, in the little third-floor sitting room.

Lambert hadn't overheard any of Mrs. Van Horne's late-supper chats with Miss Beeman. But the only sign of spine stiffening he'd seen so far was Miss Beeman's decision to get a bicycle. And that was because Mr. Carter always talked about how healthy bicycle riding was. She'd asked Lambert to teach her to ride.

He returned her smile and good morning as he slid onto his chair. He tried not to stare at the eggs, ham and fried apples in front of Frances. She hadn't touched them. She was too busy telling how she'd torn her stocking collecting spiderwebs.

From the head of the table, Lambert's mother said, "You climbed a tree, Frances, in a public park?"

Mrs. Van Horne buttered a roll and said, "It was in the interest of science, Mabel."

Lambert's stomach gurgled. He flushed with embarrassment and hoped Miss Beeman hadn't heard. Bridget set a plate like Frances's in front of him. He didn't wait for the rolls.

His mother smiled too brightly down the table. "But

surely, Frances, you don't want to become a scientist, one of those new women?"

"No, ma'am," Frances told her. "I certainly don't want to be a scientist."

Mrs. Van Horne chuckled.

Miss Beeman covered her mouth with her napkin.

Lambert's mother frowned a little, trying to decide if Frances had meant it the way it sounded. While she was distracted, Bridget passed the rolls and Lambert took two instead of the mannerly one. He shifted his milk glass to hide his butter plate.

"While we were up in the tree," Frances said, "we saw some men with a treasure map."

"If they offer you shares," said Mrs. Van Horne, "don't buy."

"Shares in what?" Mr. Carter strode in, smelling of after-shave and the pomade he used on his hair. He good-morninged everyone, asked Frances if she wasn't Carlton Ward's niece and then told Miss Beeman that he'd left a copy of the *Wheel* on the hall table. "It has an excellent article comparing bicycles according to a lady's needs. You can narrow your choice to two or three without going to every dealer in town."

Miss Beeman thanked him, then asked Lambert if he would read the article and offer suggestions. Lambert couldn't think of anything he'd rather do, after he finished the *Police Gazette*. He sneaked the newspapers to Mrs. Van Horne when he finished and he felt guilty keeping them any longer than he had to, since she paid him two cents each. Lambert got them for nothing from Mr. Carter's wastebasket.

Mr. Carter waited behind his chair until Bridget finished pouring his coffee. Then he sat beside Mrs. Van Horne and asked, "Buy shares in what, Mrs. V.?"

She said, "Captain Kidd's treasure."

Lambert choked on his eggs. Frances grinned and pounded him on the back. It was hard to glare at her when his eyes were watering.

"In my grandfather's day," Mrs. Van Horne went on, "a lot of people invested money in companies that were going to find Captain Kidd's treasure. They all had maps but none of them found a penny. My grandfather lost quite a bit of money."

Frances leaned forward. "Did anybody dig in Washington Square park?"

Mr. Carter drew in his chin and deepened his voice, his imitation of the stout, elderly councilmen at City Hall. "No digging in parks without a permit and no permit unless you're a gas or electrical company." In his own voice he added cheerfully, "Though I suspect if you offer Parks Commissioner Clauson a share of the treasure, you'll get your permit easily enough."

The dumbwaiter creaked. Bridget slid back the little door and served Mr. Carter his three-minute egg. He always called the kitchen on the speaking tube before he came down to breakfast.

"Washington Square park." He sliced the top off his boiled egg. "Right in our front yard, so to speak. We ought to dig for it ourselves."

"All you'll find is a lot of old bones," said Mrs. Van Horne. "In Kidd's day, all this"—she waved a hand—"was outside the city wall. Washington Square park was potter's field then, where they buried the criminals and the poor."

"We've had an exceptionally warm June, don't you think?" Mrs. Grew didn't consider burial arrangements a proper subject for mealtime.

"They had the gibbet over there, too." Mrs. Van Horne nodded to the front of the house. "Hung 'em and buried 'em handily." She took a roll from a staring Bridget.

"Warm and dry," Mrs. Grew said, louder. "We must water the roses by hand. Such a nuisance."

Mrs. Van Horne broke a piece from the roll and buttered it carefully. "So is having a cemetery under you. Every time people dig around here, they bring up bones. Remember when they put in the water lines, Mabel? You and I were on our way to Mr. Tiffany's and the workmen dug up . . . ."

"Bridget, pass the preserves!"

They were strawberry. Lambert took a generous helping and piled some on a piece of his second roll. Frances, he noticed, was finally eating, probably to keep from grinning. The corners of Miss Beeman's mouth twitched but her head was lowered. Lambert didn't think anyone else could see.

Mrs. Van Horne smiled. "Don't cancel your weekend cycling trip, Mr. Carter. Even if you had clear digging, you wouldn't find Kidd's treasure in Washington Square. The only place his treasure ship put in was Long Island."

Lambert stopped the sticky roll halfway to his open mouth. There *was* a treasure ... in Long Island. And if he knew bossy Frances, she'd make him go look for it.

Who was going to pay the ferry and horsecar fares? If he had to pay his own, he wouldn't be able to buy a bicycle until he was big enough to ride Mr. Carter's. Then he'd be old, too, and wouldn't need a bicycle to whiz through Biff Finnegan's territory.

He sneaked a look at Frances. She was waiting for him.

She leaned sideways and whispered, "You win, Lambie."

Lambert frowned at the bit of strawberried roll and put it in his mouth. He couldn't remember Frances saying the treasure had to be in Washington Square park, but she was sneaky enough to use that if she wanted to win. Which meant she didn't want to search Long Island; she wanted to stay around Washington Square and help Lambert detect. It was what she'd been planning right along.

"I said," Frances whispered louder, "you win."

Lambert swallowed and said, "I heard you the first time."

He didn't sound like a winner. He didn't feel like one, either. Not when he had to tell Frances that he'd made it all up, that he'd just been sweeping the steps. He'd rather run into Biff Finnegan. In a dead-end alley.

CHAPTER
FIVE

He told Frances he had to write a report.

"About the case?" She didn't wait for his nod but went right on. "Then it's part of detecting and I have to help."

"You can't. Every Pinkerton has to write his own report. Two of them," he decided, in case she planned to wait until he finished. "A daily report and one on each case, minute by minute."

They were facing each other on one of the stone benches on the stoop. Frances had her back against the house. Lambert had often sat there reading while Frances and Beth Ann played lion next door.

The railing of the basement steps had been the cage. The one playing the lion escaped from behind it and chased the other around the little, fenced front yard or through the narrow passage between the two houses. Lambert remembered a lot of howling and shrieking.

He also remembered arguments when sneaky Frances had jumped out from behind the boxwood or the wisteria instead of the cage. It made him suspicious when she

33

picked up her basket and left without an argument. He watched until she turned the corner to be sure she was gone.

Then he went inside, took Mr. Carter's bicycle magazine from the hall table and climbed the two flights of stairs to his room. He just had time to smooth the worst wrinkles from his bed covers and dig the *Police Gazette* out from under his mattress when his mother called him to go to the market with her. Nosy Frances had wasted more of his morning than he'd thought.

He rehid the newspaper and tramped back down to the entrance hall. His stomach sank as if he'd been riding an elevator when he saw his mother. She was pulling on her second-best gloves, and her hat and gown were the ones she wore for afternoon visiting.

"I'm lunching with Mrs. Sears," she told him.

That meant she was going to send him home alone with the marketing, across avenues that Biff Finnegan used, past two places where he'd already cornered Lambert.

Lambert couldn't enjoy the market the way he usually did: joking with the vendors, inspecting the live chickens and dead pheasants and doves or stopping at the fishmonger's to look for shells and sand dollars in the seaweed packed around the clams and oysters. He was too worried about the trip home. He couldn't even walk fast with two loaded baskets. He just hoped that whatever Biff was doing for the map man would take all morning.

It must have. The only scuffle Lambert had was with a pug dog wearing a big blue ribbon. It tried to eat his left shoe. Lambert had to set down the baskets and squeeze its

34

jaw joint to make it let go. Its owner, a lady as old and elegant as Mrs. Van Horne but snooty about it, gave him a quarter for catching her pet.

Lambert spent the last two blocks wondering how he could make it a steady business. Sneaky Frances probably would have thought of a way. Lambert didn't.

He added the quarter to the collar box that had been his father's. He'd get two cents for the *Police Gazette,* and Miss Beeman was going to pay him for teaching her to ride the bicycle she was going to buy. But that still left something like seventy dollars to get before he started at the new school in September.

His mind on bicycles, Lambert leafed through Mr. Carter's magazine, reading the advertisements. One showed a man wearing only a leopard skin tied on one shoulder. SANDOR THE GREAT RIDES A FOWLER was printed above his blond curls. The bulging muscles didn't look real but Lambert knew they were.

Mrs. Van Horne had seen the strong man perform at a Thirty-fourth Street theater. He really had balanced three horses on his neck and then held a grand piano, the piano stool and its player and four more musicians on top of the piano on his chest. For a hundred dollars each, Mrs. Van Horne and her friends had gone to one of Sandor's private parties. They drank champagne while Sandor walked around the room talking about muscle building and letting the ladies touch his arms. A hundred dollars just to let someone feel your muscles!

Lambert flexed his right arm and felt his biceps. Maybe if he carried enough market baskets . . . . He sighed and pulled out the *Police Gazette*. But reading about the Pinkertons made him think about sneaky Frances, so he went back to bicycles.

He was glad he did. While he was eating a sandwich in the kitchen, Miss Beeman telephoned and asked if he could meet her at the office. She was sure she could leave on time.

"And we can shop for bicycles." Her voice was tinny and wavy in the ear piece. "If you don't mind, that is."

"I want to!" Lambert told her.

He put on clean black stockings and his Sunday shoes and worked half an hour getting his part straight. He'd have to take his cap off indoors and he didn't want Miss Beeman to be ashamed of him. He wished he had pomade for his hair.

When he left, his mother was in the front hall. She'd just taken off her hat and was pushing the long hatpins back in it. She looked at Lambert's feet and hair and smiled.

"Are you returning Frances's visit?" she said.

What made her think he'd want to see bossy Frances? He held up the rolled bicycle magazine. "I'm going to help Miss Beeman choose a bicycle," he told her, and headed for the door.

"Don't be late for dinner," said his mother, warning that if Miss Beeman was late on her own account, there'd be no tray.

"We won't."

Lambert shut the front door, looked up and down the street, then ran down the steps. Not only did he have to watch for Biff and his gang, now he had to worry about passing the Ward house. It had no stoop and it wasn't the kind of house you played in front of. And not even Frances would yell out a window at him. But just in case, Lambert crossed Fifth Avenue at the corner. With the street traffic between them, he could pretend not to see or hear her. Then she'd probably come across the street to ask where he was going and invite herself along.

She didn't. And if she saw Lambert, it wasn't from any place where he could see her.

It was only two and a half blocks to Mr. Harley's law office. Once he passed the statue of Peter Stuyvesant, Lambert could stop worrying about Biff and think about bicycles. A Columbia or a Davis were his choices.

Miss Beeman bought a Fowler.

Not that the Fowler wasn't a good machine. Lambert might have put it third on his list if he'd chosen a third. But Miss Beeman seemed more interested in the poster of Sandor the Great that came with the bicycle than in frame welding and gears.

The picture was the same as the one in the advertisement but with SANDOR in fat black letters below his feet. The rest of the poster was in color and three feet long. Sandor's biceps looked like melons.

Miss Beeman said they'd collect the bicycle the next afternoon but she took the poster with her. Their ride home on the horsecar was spoiled by her worrying and fussing about crushing it. Then she asked Lambert to help put the poster on her wall. He found her some carpet tacks and said his mother needed him downstairs.

He was still grumpy in the morning and in no mood for

37

Frances Ward. But she was there before he'd finished sweeping the stoop. She walked up the side of the steps farthest from his dust, peering at the spaces in the railing.

"You ever find spiderwebs in these, Lambie?"

"Stop calling me Lambie!" The words popped out before he'd even thought them. He gripped the broom handle and waited for her to laugh and call him Lambie again. Or something worse. That's what always happened when he showed he cared.

"Why?" said Frances. She'd settled herself and her basket on a bench just as if she'd been invited. "Don't you like it?"

"What do you think?"

"I think Lambie fits you. You're little and cute."

Lambert couldn't decide if he should be pleased or insulted. Just what he'd expect from Frances Ward. He swept the stoop floor hard.

Frances swung her foot. "I don't like Bert," she said.

Lambert didn't, either. He started sweeping the steps.

"It'll just have to be Lambert, I guess."

He stopped sweeping to look over his shoulder at her. "Do you like your name?"

"Oh, yes. It suits me."

"Mine doesn't. Not inside, anyway." He went back to sweeping.

"What name fits you inside?"

Lambert had never told anyone. They'd laugh. Except that Frances didn't say what everyone else did, and she hadn't been teasing him about his name. At least, he didn't

38

think she had. And nobody had ever asked about how he felt inside.

He swept two more steps before he decided. Then he said it softly, without turning.

"Spike."

He thought she hadn't heard and was almost as sorry as relieved. Then from right behind him, she said just as softly, "Spike Grew."

She'd moved to the steps he'd just swept, either to hear better or keep anyone else from hearing. Either way, Lambert was grateful.

"Spike Grew," she said again, frowning a little.

"Le," said Lambert. "Spike LeGrew."

He flushed, mad at himself. Now he'd catch it. She'd probably just been waiting, the way she'd waited behind the boxwood next door playing lion. Lambert sneaked a look at her.

She had her elbows on her knees and her chin in her cupped hands. "Spike LeGrew," she said, no longer frowning. "Dangerous Spike LeGrew ... it sounds like a villain in a nickel thriller."

That was where Lambert had gotten it. He scowled and told her, "You shouldn't read that trash."

"Neither should you. *Gentleman* Spike LeGrew."

Lambert stopped sweeping and stared at her.

"Gentleman Spike LeGrew," she said again. "That's a name you could grow into."

Lambert flushed again, this time with pleasure. Then he wondered if she was poking fun at him after all. Before he could decide, she asked if he'd seen the map man yet.

"There isn't any treasure. Remember?" He was grumpy again, not knowing if Frances was serious about his name.

She followed him down two more steps. "But he must be doing *something* or he wouldn't be sneaking around measuring."

"Maybe he doesn't have a permit."

"We'll find out," bossy Frances decided. "If he has one, we'll know what he's doing, and if he doesn't have one, we'll know what he's doing is crooked."

Lambert wasn't going to waste the morning looking for the map man. Especially when Biff Finnegan might be with him.

He started the last step and said over his shoulder, "We don't know anything about him, not even his name."

"I thought that's what detectives were for, to find out things."

Lambert had reached the sidewalk. He turned around to see if she was laughing at him.

She sat with her elbows on the step above and her black stockinged legs stretched over the one below. Her head was tilted to one side. She was studying him the way she had the day before and it bothered him even more. Because now he knew that whatever he thought Frances Ward was going to say or do, she wouldn't.

He leaned on his broom and tried to look earnest and concerned. "I'm just thinking of you. You saw those boys he hired yesterday. Hooligans."

"They were very polite when I passed them on the path."

Lambert gave a vicious sweep with the broom. *"You're a girl."*

Frances pulled up her legs and was on her feet in one fast movement. She glared down at him, her fists jammed into her waist.

"Let me tell you something, Lambert Spike Grew! One of Mr. Pinkerton's first detectives was a woman. She caught counterfeiters and everything and she never let him down, not once! Mr. Pinkerton said so."

It was just like sneaky Frances to know something like that.

"So I can be just as good a detective as you. Maybe better!" She scooped up her basket and stomped down the last four steps. "We'll just see who finds out most about the map man the fastest."

Lambert expected her to cross the street and start looking for him in the park. But she marched past the empty house and around the corner, toward home. Lambert hoped she was mad enough to stay there.

Without Frances pestering him, he finished sweeping when Mr. Schiller was still halfway down the block. Mr. Carter's Columbia was gone from the storeroom. His bicycle club had crossed to Hoboken on the ferry last night so they could get an early start this morning. Lambert pictured them scorching down the New Jersey roads, the wind cooling their faces. Miss Beeman would probably be with them soon. Lambert didn't think he ever would.

But dogs chased bicycles. Maybe, while he was teaching Miss Beeman to ride, he could return a few more pets

41

to grateful owners. DOG CATCHER SPIKE LEGREW, DONA-
TIONS ACCEPTED.

Miss Beeman worked a half-day on Saturdays. She
planned to pick up the bicycle in the afternoon and learn to
ride it on the way home. Lambert was waiting on the
stoop when she came home to change. She'd shortened an
old skirt for bicycle riding. It wasn't until she was back
downstairs that she remembered she had to walk to
Broadway and then ride the cable car uptown in an ankle-
length skirt.

"I can't!" she cried. "What will people think?"

Lambert's mother and Mrs. Van Horne were having
lemonade in the parlor. They came into the front hall,
fanning themselves.

"That's a very practical length," said Mrs. Van Horne.

"For bicycle riding," said Miss Beeman. She was almost
in tears. Lambert wanted to pat her hand. "People will
excuse it if I have a bicycle, but I can't walk the street like
this."

Lambert's mother nodded agreement.

"Nonsense," said Mrs. Van Horne. "Members of my
Rainy Day Club wear skirts shorter than that. Some wear
them even when there isn't a cloud."

Mrs. Grew sniffed. "New women."

"Young women, Mabel. Professional women like Miss
Beeman." Mrs. Van Horne snapped her fan shut. "I have
an engagement uptown. I shall leave early and accompany
you."

She swept into her suite, her afternoon gown trailing

42

behind her. Lambert wished she'd telephoned the livery stable first. It would have saved time.

But Mrs. Van Horne didn't drive them in her carriage. She rode the cable car with them, wearing her rainy day skirt, which was two inches shorter than Miss Beeman's.

The Rainy Day Club rules said six to eight inches above the ground, and Mrs. Van Horne thought the shorter skirt length made the point better. She pinned a blue ribbon on Miss Beeman's shirtwaist like the one she wore. It had EXPERIENTIA DOCET written on it in silver letters. The club emblem, a silver umbrella, dangled from the ribbon.

"But I'm not a . . . ." started Miss Beeman.

"An *honorary* member," Mrs. Van Horne told her, and swept her out the door and down the steps with a funny account of how the club motto had been chosen. Mrs. Van Horne had wanted SANITY IN DRESS or at least EXPERI-ENCE TEACHES in plain English.

On the cable car she entertained them with stories about the places they passed or the things that had been there before. She stayed on the car when Lambert helped Miss Beeman off at Forty-eighth Street, smiling and waving to them as long as they could see her.

There were always men loafing at bicycle shops. Today, because of the heat, they were sitting on boxes in front of the store. Miss Beeman insisted on getting out of their sight before starting her lesson. Lambert walked her toward Fifth Avenue, which didn't have quite as much traffic up here as the other avenues.

Miss Beeman didn't need much teaching; she had a

43

good sense of balance. After a half-hour on the bicycle, she could have ridden it straight home as planned, with Lambert taking the horsecar, if she'd had the avenue to herself. But traffic panicked her. Any passing carriage or wagon, even a messenger boy on his bicycle, sent her swerving blindly. Drivers yelled and cussed. Twice she ran into the curb and would have fallen if Lambert hadn't been trotting alongside to catch her.

At four-thirty they were only as far as Madison Square. Lambert was hot, thirsty and exhausted. Miss Beeman didn't look any better. She stood beside her bicycle and fanned herself with a crumpled handkerchief.

"Let's get a drink and rest awhile," she said.

They crossed the street and walked along the park to the Madison Avenue corner where there was a drinking fountain. There was also a big ornamental fountain. Children splashed in it until the policeman chased them. Before the blue coat and helmet were out of sight, they were back in the water. Lambert envied them. The line at the drinking fountain was a long one. It wasn't the first time Lambert had thought "ladies first" was unfair.

After he finally got a drink, he splashed water over his head. Most of it ran down his back, but his shirt was so sweat soaked it didn't matter.

"There's a hokey-pokey man," said Miss Beeman. She pushed a dime into Lambert's hand. "If you get us each one, I'll try to find an empty bench."

Lambert grinned and thanked her. The man was selling hokey-pokeys as fast as he could take them out of the box he carried by a strap over his shoulder. Lambert was afraid there wouldn't be any left when it was his turn. But he handed over the dime and got two slices of pink, white and brown striped ice cream wrapped in paper.

He found Miss Beeman fanning herself with the handkerchief and rocking. A line of rocking chairs stood on one side of the path. She'd leaned the bicycle against one to save it for Lambert but she needn't have bothered. There were plenty of empty chairs, though the benches that still lined the other side of the path were crowded.

"I don't understand why," Miss Beeman whispered. "These chairs are much nicer. I believe I'll write a letter to the parks commissioner and thank him. What did Mr. Carter say his name was?"

"Mr. Clauson," Lambert told her.

They rocked and ate ice cream until a fellow the size of Biff Finnegan stopped in front of them. He wore a gray uniform and had a black satchel slung over his shoulder like the hokey-pokey man.

He held his hand out to Miss Beeman and said, "That's ten cents, ma'am."

"We've already paid," Miss Beeman told him.

"Then I have to see your tickets." His hand was still out.

Miss Beeman looked at Lambert, surprised. "Did the hokey-pokey man give you tickets?"

"For the chairs, ma'am," said the uniformed tough. "So I know you already paid for the chairs."

Miss Beeman stopped rocking. "This is a public park," she told him.

45

"Yes, ma'am. But the chairs ain't. They belong to Mr. Spake and Mr. Spake charges five cents for sittin' in 'em."

"Five cents!"

"If you don't wanna pay that, you can move to the ones that don't have arms. They're only three cents." His hand was still out for the money and the gray uniform was looking bigger by the second to Lambert.

"I don't want to pay one cent," said Miss Beeman.

The hand became a fist and the thumb jerked over his shoulder. "Then you gotta go sit on the benches."

"But they're in the sun! Besides, there isn't any room."

"They givin' you trouble, Ned?" Another gray uniform with a black satchel came up. The face under the visor was familiar. Lambert had seen it yesterday with Biff Finnegan.

He gulped the last of his ice cream and got ready to run.

CHAPTER SIX

A sudden sharp pain shot through Lambert's eyes. He rocked forward, his hands pressed over them. Miss Beeman leaned over him, asking what was wrong. She sounded frightened.

"I ate the ice cream too fast," he told her. "I'll be all right. Just put my hand on the bicycle seat and I can follow."

He kept his head down and his free hand over his eyes long after the pain was gone. When he risked a look, Miss Beeman was leading him out of the Fifth Avenue side of the park. They stood on the paving stones and tried to decide what to do.

Lambert offered to ride the bicycle home while Miss Beeman took the horsecar. He didn't often get a chance to ride a bicycle, and those he could borrow were usually too big for him. So was Miss Beeman's Fowler. But it was a girl's bicycle with no crossbar. He could stand on the pedals. It would be hard and risky in all the traffic and he'd rather not be seen on it, but he was willing to chance it.

Miss Beeman's lessons had frightened her too much to let him try. "No," she said, "it's too dangerous. We'll walk. Unless you're in a hurry and want to go ahead?"

He didn't. They took turns walking the machine and stopped to look in store windows, joking or admiring. It gave Lambert a very grown-up feeling.

It was time to dress for dinner when they reached Washington Square. Lambert took the bicycle down to the basement, put it in Mr. Carter's stand and gave it a dusting. It really was a good machine.

He was going to stop in the kitchen and beg something to eat but he heard Bridget and Molly giggling over the Sandor poster. He turned and went back to the inside stairs, feeling short and skinny and not at all grown up. Sandor the Great would have carried the bicycle home, with Miss Beeman on it. Lambert couldn't even have protected her from Mr. Spake's bullies.

Before he reached his room, his mother called. Nosy Frances was at the front door. She must have seen them wheeling the bicycle past her house. Lambert was glad he hadn't been riding it.

His mother was standing in the hall, worrying. "I invited her in," she told Lambert, "but she refused. It's much cooler inside with the windows closed and the curtains drawn. And the sun will ruin her complexion."

"I'll tell her," Lambert promised, but the first thing he said to Frances was, "Mister Spake!"

At the same time, Frances said, "Tully Spake!" It ruined his victory. Hers, too, from the way she frowned.

"How'd you know?" she said.

She didn't have her basket with her and she looked even neater than she did in the mornings. She was sitting in Lambert's place, her back against the wall, her legs stretched out in front of her on the bench. Lambert sat at the other end, put one knee on the bench and swung the other foot.

"I don't reveal my sources," he told her.

"Well, I don't mind telling you mine: Commissioner Clauson."

Lambert stopped swinging his foot. "He told *you?*"

Frances nodded, pleased with herself. "I just telephoned his house when I knew he wouldn't be there and said, 'Would you please ask the commissioner to telephone Carlton Ward?' and when he did, I told him Uncle Carlton wasn't home now but he wanted to know if some man had a permit for what he was doing in the parks." Frances grinned. "He knew exactly who I meant and said it was perfectly legal, that Mr. Tully Spake had a permit to install chairs in the city parks at his own expense."

"Rocking chairs," Lambert added. "And he's charging people to sit in them."

"How did you find that out?"

"Undercover work." He certainly wasn't going to tell her about Miss Beeman leading him away from Biff's pal and out of the park. An ice cream pain didn't last very long, and a gentleman was supposed to protect a lady at all costs. Frances would never call him Gentleman Spike LeGrew again. He'd be Lambie forever.

Frances said something but all he caught was, "How about you, Spike?"

He pulled a leaf off the wisteria vine and scowled at it. How could she call him that now? It just made him *feel* like a Lambie-pambie.

"I said," Frances repeated, "I figure it's a tie."

She meant their test to see who was the better detective. She counted off their points on her fingers. Lambert pulled green stuff from the leaf, trying to get a perfect skeleton. Maybe he'd start a collection. Collecting leaf skeletons was the kind of thing a Lambie did.

It made as much sense as Frances collecting spiderwebs. But then she only said she did. It was probably only an excuse to go nosing into other people's private business. Why else would she want them?

Before he could ask, Frances said, "What's our next case, Spike? Something exciting, I hope. Mr. Spake certainly wasn't."

"Most detective work isn't," Lambert told his leaf skeleton, though he'd never read anything about the Pinkertons that wasn't. Except writing reports. Mr. Pinkerton insisted on detailed reports. Lambert was reminding Frances about them when his mother stepped outside and asked if her uncle was expecting her for dinner.

Frances didn't get up but she scrooched around to sit properly. Lambert couldn't help noticing that Frances didn't have to sit on the edge of the bench for her feet to touch the stoop floor.

"Good evening, ma'am," she said. "My uncle is visiting up the Hudson this week."

Mrs. Grew smiled. "Then perhaps you would like to dine with us?"

Lambert tossed the mangled leaf over his shoulder. That's why Frances was so neat. She'd come dressed for dinner, planning to wheedle an invitation.

His mother said she'd have to telephone Mrs. Ridge, but Lambert knew what the answer would be. From what he heard in the kitchen, Lambert didn't think Mr. Ward's housekeeper would be part of one of Frances's schemes. But from what he knew firsthand about Frances, he figured Mrs. Ridge would be relieved to have her gone for the evening.

Mrs. Van Horne invited Frances to use her bathroom to tidy up. Lambert went upstairs to change. When he came down, Frances was sitting in the parlor with the ladies.

The sun was down and his mother had opened the windows to catch the evening breeze. If there was one, it wasn't strong enough to get inside. Ladies were lucky. They didn't have to wear jackets and could use fans.

Mrs. Van Horne shook hers vigorously. "And to think I could be in Saratoga," she said.

Nosy Frances asked, politely, why she wasn't.

"My brother-in-law is giving the Fourth of July speech at the Battery," she said. "I've been invited to sit on the platform beside his wife. I didn't expect this heat when I accepted. However" —the corners of her mouth twitched— "it will be worth it when the day comes. Cornelius isn't the only one who can use the platform for political purposes."

Before Frances could get a question out, Mrs. Grew stood and announced dinner, even though Bridget hadn't finished setting the table.

51

Frances went to the place next to Lambert's as if she belonged there. Pretty soon she'd have her own napkin ring. With Mr. Carter away, Lambert had to pull out chairs for all the ladies. He made Frances wait until last, but she didn't seem to care.

Bridget scurried around with bowls of chilled soup, while Lambert's mother began the dinner conversation by asking Miss Beeman if she found bicycling pleasant.

"Not yet." And from the sound of her voice, Miss Beeman didn't think she ever would. "When you're on a bicycle, the traffic is so . . . so confusing." Then she straightened and said, "But when we stopped to rest at Madison Square, the strangest thing happened."

She was better at changing subjects than Lambert's mother. The rocking chairs and uniformed collectors interested everyone, especially Frances. Now she knew Lambert had learned about Mr. Spake by accident.

Lambert sneaked a look. She was smiling. She'd probably laugh out loud when she heard about him letting Miss Beeman lead him away from Biff's pal.

But Miss Beeman didn't get that far. Mrs. Van Horne began wondering if Mr. Spake was going to put rocking chairs across the street in Washington Square park. Then Mrs. Grew worried that rented chairs might be un-American.

"Please don't mention it to Cornelius," said Mrs. Van Horne. "He'll add another half-hour to his speech."

Lambert's mother looked as stricken as if she were already standing in the sun to listen. "I do hope this heat breaks before then," she said. "It's the warmest June the weather bureau has recorded."

"A drive would be refreshing. I'll order the carriage and we'll go to Maillard's for ice cream. It's the perfect dessert on an evening like this."

Maillard's was in the basement of the Fifth Avenue Hotel and the hotel was on Madison Square. Lambert and Miss Beeman had come out of the park across the street from it.

Frances leaned toward Lambert and whispered, "I bet we go at least once around Madison Square."

Lambert smiled and tried to look superior. Mrs. Van Horne almost never ate dessert. He'd known right away that she wanted to see the chairs and collectors.

He was disappointed when Miss Beeman asked to be excused from the outing. "I'm much too tired," she apologized. She even refused the lemon trifle Mrs. Magee had prepared for dessert. Lambert had been all ready to say he'd have some, too, just to keep her company. He should have remembered that things came in threes and not asked Miss Beeman about another lesson after church.

"I don't think so, Lambert," she said. "I'm sure I'll still be very tired."

It was the worst of the three disappointments. But as she left the table, Miss Beeman put a hand on his shoulder, smiled down at him and said, "I am very thankful you were with me today, Lambert. I would never have managed without you."

He could still feel her hand when he and Frances went out on the stoop to wait for the carriage. He wished Frances would excuse herself, too, especially when she started giving him advice about Miss Beeman's lessons.

"You should take her down to Canal Street on a week-day," she said.

"You're loony," he told her. "That's the worst traffic in New York City."

"I know. Once she rides through that, traffic won't scare her anymore. You have to stand up to your fears; face the very worst."

Lambert wished he could tell her about Biff Finnegan.

She stood up. "Is that Mrs. Van Horne's carriage?"

It was. Lambert went in to tell her it had arrived. When he came out with the ladies, Frances was talking to Otto, Mrs. Van Horne's coachman.

She was probably telling him that if he stood up to the teamsters when they tried to cut him off, he'd stop being afraid of their huge wagons and six-horse hitches. Lambert agreed; Otto would have other things to worry about in a hospital.

He and Frances were given the seat facing backward. Otto had put the top down, but if there was a breeze, the buildings cut it off. And they couldn't drive fast enough to make one. Everyone in New York seemed to be looking for a cooler spot. A horsecar passed them with men standing on the steps as well as the platform. A pair of toddlers waved from a window. They giggled and hid their faces when Lambert and Frances waved back. They

54

were the only ones on the horsecar who didn't look hot and tired.

When Lambert saw Madison Square, he was glad that Miss Beeman hadn't come with them. The traffic was much worse than it had been in the afternoon. Otto circled the square so he could drive back down Fifth Avenue and stop in front of the hotel. They passed the fountains but were on the wrong side of the street with too many wagons and carriages between. Lambert only glimpsed the very top of the large fountain. They couldn't see any chairs or collectors, either. But they heard somebody in the park yell an insult.

Lambert grinned. It sounded as if Biff Finnegan and his pals were on the receiving end for a change. Then he saw light from street lamps glinting on clusters of police helmets at every path. Laughter had followed the insult, but Lambert noticed three of the high-domed helmets vanish under the trees. He hoped Mrs. Van Horne wasn't thinking of walking through the park.

If she had been, she changed her mind. Except for traffic tie-ups, the carriage didn't stop until it drew up in front of the hotel. Lambert scrambled out first so he could hand down the ladies—Frances, too. She put her hand out and he had to take it, though he didn't know why an ace tree climber needed help getting out of a carriage.

They weren't the only ones turning down the three steps to Maillard's Confectionery, and there were only two empty tables. A young lady in a long white apron led them to the one under a high window. Frances asked Mrs. Van

Horne if she could have an ice cream soda, strawberry. Lambert asked for a soda, too, but chocolate. The ladies ordered dishes of strawberry ice cream.

Lambert glanced around the busy room. Maillard's was famous for its sculptures of chocolate and spun-sugar elegancies. He'd hoped to see some, but the counters at the back of the room were bare.

"Where's the candy?" he finally asked.

"In the other shop." Mrs. Van Horne nodded to a door on the opposite side of the entrance steps. "It's closed this evening."

"This heat probably melted the chocolate," said Lambert's mother. She was smiling dreamily. "Fred always brought me something from Maillard's on my birthday."

She was trying to get Lambert to remember a wreath of pink sugar roses when the waitress brought their order. As she served them, there was a sudden lull in the traffic noise and they heard yelling in the park. Their waitress looked up at the open window.

Another waitress, passing their table, told her, "Ought to throw those chairs in the East River."

"Oh, dear," murmured Lambert's mother.

"You were right, Mabel," said Mrs. Van Horne. "It seems paying for chairs in a park is not considered American."

Frances grinned happily over her soda glass. "Maybe we'll have a New York Boston Tea Party."

"Pink ice cream!" Mrs. Grew said brightly. The dish being slid in front of her and talking about the past had reminded her of a more suitable subject for conversation.

"You and Mama used to take me for ice cream. Some place with a fountain with goldfish in it. I always asked for pink ice cream."

It was more interesting than the weather. Lambert listened as he started on his soda.

Mrs. Van Horne frowned at a spoonful of ice cream. "A goldfish fountain?"

Mrs. Grew nodded. "And the ice cream always came with two little cakes tied with a pink ribbon. I saved all the ribbons for my doll."

"Oh." Mrs. Van Horne smiled and ate the spoonful of ice cream. "That was Berk's. Imagine you remembering that. You couldn't have been more than five or six. But the fountain wasn't in Berk's. It was in the subway station. Mr. Beach's Pneumatic Subway."

Now Lambert's mother frowned, trying to remember.

"Subway?" said Lambert.

"Underground," said Frances, forgetting her soda for a minute. "Did it run, Mrs. Van Horne?"

"Of course. That was the reason we went to Berk's so often that summer, to ride Mr. Beach's subway. It was very elegant, with potted palms and fountains in the stations. The car looked a little odd, though. It had to be round to fit the tunnel because Beach used enormous fans to blow it back and forth under Fifth Avenue."

Frances looked at Lambert, asking if she could believe that. Lambert nodded without letting go of his straw. Mrs. Van Horne might decorate her stories, but they were always true.

"Why isn't it still running?" said Frances.

57

"It probably didn't make any money," Lambert told her.

"But it did," said Mrs. Van Horne. "A hundred thousand dollars, if I remember correctly, in just a year."

"A hundred thousand dollars?" Frances sounded doubtful.

"People liked to ride it. There was always a line. Mr. Beach put a piano in the Washington Square station to entertain them." Mrs. Van Horne's mouth twitched. "Surely you remember that, Mabel. You always wanted the pianist to play 'Little Brown Jug' so you could shout the ho-ho-ho's."

Lambert stared at his mother, but she busied herself with her dish of ice cream. Lambert couldn't picture his mother singing in a station, not even as a little girl. It was easier to imagine Frances as a proper lady worrying what the neighbors would say. Especially after the way she was acting tonight: wanting to be handed out of carriages and sitting prim and proper with her left hand on her lap and not tipping her glass even though the soda . . . . Lambert dropped his straw. The level was even lower in his own glass. He'd almost embarrassed his mother by making a slurping noise with his straw. He glared at Frances, but she was busy listening to the story of Mr. Beach's subway.

". . . such a short distance," Mrs. Van Horne was saying. "And he couldn't get permits to expand. So after a year, he closed down the stations and gave all the money to charity."

A hundred thousand dollars! Mr. Beach must have

been loony. Or the city council had been for not letting him expand. A hundred thousand dollars a *year!*

His mother said, "But they gave that man with the chairs a permit."

"That makes two mistakes," said Mrs. Van Horne.

She'd talked so much that her ice cream had melted. But when she signaled the waitress, it was to ask for the check. Lambert watched Frances finish her soda.

He'd had to leave some of his, so as not to make a rude noise. But Frances had saved some ice cream for last. After she'd spooned it out, her glass was practically empty. Lambert had to admit she was good at planning things. He guessed you had to be if you were sneaky.

Otto was waiting to help the ladies into the carriage. Lambert went to look in the candy shop window. He was surprised that Frances didn't tag along, but she didn't miss anything. The windows were curtained. She didn't grin or nudge him, either, when Mrs. Van Horne told Otto, "We'll drive around the park."

Otto drove around the hotel block first, so when he turned the last corner they were rolling along the north side of the square. He cut off a carriage and a billboard wagon to get next to the park. The only unusual noise now was whooping and cheering ahead of them, where the fountains were.

His mother said, "Whatever it was seems to have been settled."

But Lambert, riding backward, saw a gray uniform run from the park to a pair of policemen. He turned to Frances, but she was studying Mrs. Van Horne with her head cocked to one side. Lambert looked past the ladies again. The policemen were running in their direction, rattling their clackers for help. Lambert saw why when the carriage turned the corner.

People were milling around the big fountain, shouting encouragement and getting in the way of police. Then somebody lifted a struggling gray uniform and tossed the collector into the fountain. The cheers were deafening. As they drove past, the man who'd done the tossing stepped onto the fountain rim, turned toward the crowd and lifted his arms. Lambert saw him clearly in the lamplight. Except for the suit, he looked just like the poster in Miss Beeman's room.

CHAPTER
SEVEN

Lambert's brain wouldn't turn off and let him go to sleep. Pictures came and went the way they did in a stereopticon: Miss Beeman wobbling along on her bicycle, Mr. Spake's collectors looming over them with their black satchels, Sandor (if it really was Sandor the Great) proud in the center of the cheering crowd and, worst of all, Frances with her head tipped to one side and not saying anything except her thank-you's all the way home.

Lambert groaned, turned onto his back and threw his arms straight out. It was no cooler that way. He rolled off the bed, bunched up the coverlet, grabbed a pillow and padded downstairs. He was still short enough to fit on a stoop bench.

The front door was standing open. Lambert stood in the hall and listened. Someone was singing across the street . . . "The Sidewalks of New York." In weather like this, the parks were open all night. Angry voices told the singer to shut his trap. From just outside the door, his mother's voice wondered what would happen when Mr. Spake put his chairs in Washington Square park.

"We don't know that he will, Mabel," said Mrs. Van Horne. "And from what we saw tonight, he has his hands full in Madison Square."

"But if he does and if the heat doesn't break . . . . "

Tempers would run short and there'd be a lot more people in the park, most of whom couldn't afford to pay for a chair. And some of those who could were sure to get angry if they had to pay for sitting in a public park.

As if following his thoughts, Mrs. Van Horne said, "Miss Beeman said half the benches are still in place. And that crowd tonight didn't seem angry. They treated it more as a lark."

"All the same," said Lambert's mother, "I wish the second floor were still fully occupied."

Lambert knew she wasn't thinking of the money this time. But Mr. Quince, who'd gone to Florida, was as old as Mrs. Van Horne and frail besides. And the "gentleman" who'd left owing money probably would have skedaddled through the basement and over the back fence at the first sign of trouble. And Lambert . . . what would he do?

He hoisted his pillow and coverlet and went back upstairs. He'd rather not sleep if he was going to have nightmares about fighting rioters off the stoop. Halfway up the second flight, it occurred to him that the rioters wouldn't want to get in the house unless Biff's pals were inside. But dreaming about trying to keep *them* out wasn't any improvement.

Frances must have had trouble sleeping, too. She didn't

come around until Lambert had finished sweeping and was trying to ride Miss Beeman's bicycle around the storeroom. He flushed when Molly caught him.

"Frances Ward is at the door," she told him.

"Tell her I'm indisposed."

"I can't do that, Lambert!"

"You do it for Mrs. Van Horne."

"Mrs. Van Horne is a lady." Molly's tone said that only ladies were allowed to be indisposed. "Besides, your ma wouldn't like it."

Which was probably why sneaky Frances had waited until she could knock on the door and ask for him. He stood the Fowler between two of Mrs. Van Horne's trunks. Mr. Carter would be home this evening and need his stand.

As he passed the kitchen, Mrs. Magee called, "Let me know quick if she's staying to breakfast."

"She isn't." She'd have to go home and change for Sunday school. Unless she was already dressed for church.

She wasn't. And she had her basket with her, too. She saw him leaving the basement and came down the front steps to meet him.

Lambert leaned his back against the railing, crossed his arms and tensed them to make his biceps bulge. He watched his right sleeve from the corner of his eye. It didn't stir. He sighed and asked Frances what she wanted, but softly. His mother hadn't closed the windows yet.

"Spiderwebs," Frances told him. "Uncle Carlton's coming home tomorrow and he'll want to see at least one."

"I thought you were the one who liked spiderwebs."

63

"I don't *like* them," said Frances. "I *need* them. For my summer project."

Lambert sat down beside her on the steps. "I'm glad I'm out of that school if they're giving summer projects now."

"It isn't for school." Frances rummaged in her basket. "I'm something of a problem for Uncle Carlton. The only thing he knows about children is the way Grandfather raised him and Daddy. Their tutor made them choose summer projects so I have to choose one."

"A real project? With reports ... ?"

"And graphs and Latin labels." Frances found what she was looking for ... a linen-wrapped bundle.

"That's cheesy," Lambert told her. "*Double* cheesy."

"Yes, but Uncle Carlton only knows the rules for boys, so I can do lots of things Beth Ann can't."

She folded back the corners of the napkin and offered thick slices of Dundee cake. He took one to be polite. It was even staler than the scones had been.

Frances said, "If I'd known about the detecting sooner, I could have made that my project. I have to write the reports anyhow."

"Switch," Lambert said before he thought. To his relief, Frances said she couldn't.

"'A summer project,'" she chanted, "'instills resourcefulness, industry and stick-to-itiveness.'"

"Then collect them all and finish."

Frances shook her head. "A project ends the last day of August with"—she chanted again—"'proof of a reasonable application each week.'" In normal tones, she added, "And I already used the excuse that I couldn't find any perfect ones, so I absolutely have to have one or two tomorrow."

Frances was busy with her basket again. She poured water from a jar into two smaller ones. The water turned white. She dropped two bent tubes into the jars and handed one to Lambert.

"It's only watercolor so don't worry about it washing off."

Lambert tried to think of one good reason why he couldn't go over to the park.

Bossy Frances shoved squares of black paper in his other hand. "You remember what to do, don't you? Come on."

Since she headed for the empty house next door, Lambert went along.

"There hasn't been anyone around here for a week, so there should be lots of spiderwebs. You go around back," she bossed, "and I'll hunt out here. Only perfect ones, remember."

The passage between the houses was so narrow that Lambert's house, which had been built later, had no windows on that side. Nothing grew there except moss. But when Lambert stepped into the backyard, right in front of him was a bush with a perfect web.

He crouched in front of it and held up the paint jar. When he blew in one end of the crooked tube, paint came out the other, just as Frances had told him. Only she hadn't said it sprayed everything for two feet around. No wonder the gardener wouldn't let her collect in Mr. Ward's garden.

He inched a square of black paper up behind the painted web. When he pulled it forward, the web stuck the instant it touched paper. Only it wasn't centered. If Frances said anything, he'd tell her he'd done it on purpose to leave room for the Latin names.

He hadn't thought to take his penknife out. He had to fish it from his pocket and open it one handed. After he cut the spokes from the bush, he sat back on his heels and admired the white web on the black paper. Then he stood up to look for another and saw the dirt.

CHAPTER EIGHT

When Lambert came out of the passage, Frances was reaching behind a paint-spattered boxwood. She drew out a square of black paper with a web so off center it hung over one side.

"Dangnation!" she said.

Lambert handed her the one he'd mounted. He hoped his smile looked superior. If it did, Frances missed it.

She said, "Thanks, I can use this if you show me where you found it," all the while rummaging in her basket for a tape measure, pencil and a wrinkled bit of paper. "I need the distance from the ground, the name of the bush, the weather and time of day."

Lambert followed her through the passage. "You want the spider, too?"

"Not if I have to catch and kill it."

Lambert grinned. He had a matchbox in his room. All he needed was the spider. Then the next time Frances came around, she wouldn't stay long.

But Frances added, "Spiders are useful creatures. I did

67

my first summer project about one I kept in my room."

With the white paint, she didn't need Lambert to point out the bush. When he caught up, she was hunkered down measuring from the ground to what she guessed was the center of the web. She hadn't noticed the dirt and when Lambert pointed it out, she just shrugged.

"Somebody bought the house and is having some gardening done."

Lambert shook his head. "No gardener did that. It's fresh dirt, piled on top. Look at the end of the border. It's nearly two feet high there. It'll kill those shrubs."

He knew that much from his mother fussing over her rose bushes. Frances was still making notes on her scrap of paper. Lambert grabbed a handful of the fresh dirt and scattered it on a path worn in the grass.

"Look," he said. "It's a different color."

Frances frowned at it a moment, then looked at Lambert and said, "Are there any bones?"

"Bones?"

She opened her mouth, but whatever she was going to say was stopped by the clank of the little iron gate at the front of the house. Lambert remembered something. Two somethings.

"We have to get out," he whispered fiercely.

They couldn't use the passage. Nor the house, even if it wasn't locked and it probably was. The gate to the alley at the end of the lot was kept locked, too. But the gate was in the drying yard and the yard had a six-foot board fence to hide drying laundry. It would hide them, too, until the men left.

Lambert headed for the opening in the fence, but Frances grabbed a handful of shirt and pulled him back.

"They'll know somebody's here from the paint," she whispered. "Get the basket. Come on . . . wait."

She took back the mounted webs that she'd put on top. Then, one in each hand, she started for the front yard, chattering over her shoulder to Lambert.

"You'd think we'd improve with practice, wouldn't you? This one's no good at all, *absolutely* no good. But maybe we can use this one. We can put an early date on it and be finished. He'll never know. What do you think, Spike?"

"That's cheating." And not what a Spike would say, but it was all Lambert could think of with two big men eyeing them as they came out of the passage. Heavy tool bags lay beside the sprayed boxwood and when one of the men moved back toward the gate, Lambert could hardly breathe. But Frances put Lambert's web back in the basket, right side up, and kept going.

The man opened the gate for her. She thanked him with a smile. Lambert nodded, not trusting his voice, and hurried after her toward Fifth Avenue. Behind him, the gate clanked shut. He wanted to know what the men were doing but if he looked back, they'd know he was suspicious of them.

Frances had torn her web into bits. She skipped ahead of Lambert, tossed the black pieces into the air and twirled under them. When she fell into step beside Lambert, she was laughing and her excitement wasn't acting.

"They've gone into the basement," she told him.

"They're digging down there, aren't they? I was right, wasn't I? It *is* treasure!"

She had it all figured. Mr. Spake's rocking chairs were just an excuse so he could measure Washington Square park to see where the treasure was buried.

"Only he can't dig in a park," she finished, "so he's digging a tunnel from Beth Ann's old house."

"All the way under the street?"

"Mr. Beach dug a lot farther than that."

"That was for a subway."

Frances nodded. "Yes, I think it was. Last night I was sure he'd found the treasure, the way he stopped digging and gave all that money away."

"You heard Mrs. Van Horne . . . . "

"I know, but digging a subway would have been the very best cover. Only Mr. Spake wouldn't be going to all this trouble if he didn't know the treasure was still there."

Lambert groaned.

They'd slowed their pace as they turned the corner, but now Frances stopped completely to stare at a white-uniformed man pushing a wide broom along the curb. She was watching the street cleaner, but she was thinking about Mr. Spake because she said, "Do you think Mr. Spake started that trouble last night so nobody will notice what he's doing down here?"

"He isn't doing anything down here," Lambert reminded her.

"He will." Frances moved slowly toward her uncle's house. "He has a permit for all the parks . . . . "

"Cover," Lambert said, and nodded in an exaggerated way.

"Yes, and he wouldn't start on the one that's really important." She turned and walked backward, facing Lambert. "Maybe it's Captain Kidd's treasure! Think of it, Spike! Gold doubloons and pieces of eight and pearls the size of pigeon eggs in musty trunks and old sail canvas bags."

It sounded like *Dick O'Dare and the Barbary Pirates*. So did her story about how Captain Kidd's treasure had gotten under Washington Square park: One of the pirates who'd helped bury it had come back and moved it.

"To potter's field," said Lambert.

If Frances noticed the sarcasm, she ignored it. "A cemetery's a dandy place to hide treasure," she said. "People are always digging there and he could get at it when he needed more. And that's why none of those companies ever found it. Spike"—she stared at him intently—"we have to see how far they've dug. There's no sense closing in until they find the treasure, but we have to keep tabs on them."

Lambert wished her uncle knew more about raising girls. If he did, Frances wouldn't be so loony about pirates and treasure.

He told her, "I'm going to miss breakfast if I don't hurry." He backed a step. Then, in case she was thinking of inviting herself again, added, "And Miss Beeman may want another riding lesson before Sunday school."

"Can you come over tonight for a late supper?"

Lambert hadn't expected *her* to invite *him* and if he

71

had, it wouldn't have been for Sunday night supper. While he searched for an excuse (maybe Mr. Carter coming home from his bicycle trip), Frances tugged the basket from his hand, said, "I'll have Mrs. Ridge telephone your mother," and ran up the steps. She grinned and waved before the wide door opened and she stepped inside.

Lambert grinned and waved back. Frances could get the housekeeper to telephone his mother and his mother would accept the invitation and make Lambert go. But Frances didn't know that he had to go home when the street lamps were lit. There'd be no sneaking around Beth Ann's old yard tonight.

All the same, he wanted to be there when Mrs. Ridge telephoned, just in case he thought of a way to stop his mother from accepting the invitation. He hurried back around the corner, forcing himself not to look at the not-quite-empty house.

He was so sure he'd find his mother talking into the telephone that he just stared at Bridget when she warned him to hurry and asked if he wanted Corn Flakes or Shredded Wheat. She repeated the question impatiently.

"Corn Flakes, please," Lambert said and ran upstairs.

He used the second-floor bathroom so he could hear the telephone. With Mr. Carter coming back tonight, Molly and Bridget would have to clean it tomorrow anyhow. He was smoothing his hair when two longs and a short jangled. Lambert gave the roller towel a pull to hide the used place, remembered to yank the toilet chain and ran for the stairs.

His mother had already picked up the receiver. Lambert leaned over the banister and listened to her I'm-not-so-sure's change to he'd-be-delighted's. She was smiling when she put the receiver back on the pronged hook.

"Lambert," she said brightly, "that was Mrs. Ridge, Mr. Ward's housekeeper. She'd like you to help Frances collect her webs."

"I already did."

His mother nodded. "Yes, Mrs. Ridge told me. But these are webs of night spiders."

"*Night* spiders?"

"I suppose they catch moths." Mrs. Grew checked her pompadour in the gilt-framed mirror and tucked in a strand. "Frances is nervous about going into the garden alone at night and Mrs. Ridge isn't fond of spiders. I can't say I blame her. So she asked if you'd escort Frances tonight and help her."

Lambert had to admire Frances. She not only had flummoxed Mrs. Ridge into inviting him, she'd gotten the housekeeper to think it was her idea.

Mrs. Grew headed back to the dining room. "Come to breakfast now, Lambert. We've already started. You can pack after church."

"*Pack?*"

"Since you'll be up late," his mother said over her shoulder, "Mrs. Ridge has kindly asked you to stay overnight."

Sneaky Frances had also taken care of the rule about streetlights.

CHAPTER NINE

Lambert hadn't been mistaken; it was Sandor the Great who'd tossed Mr. Spake's collector into the fountain. The story was on the front pages of most of the newspapers. But no newspapermen had been in Madison Square when it happened, so the stories were all hearsay and different. Lambert hardly had his chair pulled out before Miss Beeman was asking for his first-hand account.

He gave it but, hard as he tried, there was no way he could not make Sandor sound like a hero. Especially to Miss Beeman, who'd been bullied by the collectors.

She sighed and said wistfully, "I wish I'd gone with you."

"He'll probably do an encore tonight," said Mrs. Van Horne. "And this time his manager will be certain there are newspapermen around to see."

Miss Beeman sat straighter and, to Lambert's surprise, said, "I don't think that's very kind." She said it gently, but it was the closest Lambert had ever heard her come to a criticism.

"But practical," Mrs. Van Horne said cheerfully. "It's almost impossible to get people into a theater in this heat." She waved Molly and the coffeepot away. "Sandor's New York appearance may come to an abrupt end."

Maybe *he'd* started the trouble in Madison Square. Lambert didn't really think so, but it was something to put up against Frances Ward's ninnyhammer ideas about pirate treasure.

When he was half-finished with his cereal, Miss Beeman handed him another surprise: She asked for another riding lesson. After the first one, Lambert hadn't expected her to take the machine out of the basement except to sell it. A second lesson would put him closer to a bicycle of his own. He ate as fast as he dared, worried that she would change her mind again.

All she needed was encouragement and not much of that. She rode up and down the street by herself and then around the block. She stopped in front of Lambert, one boot on the curb to hold up her bicycle.

"You're a natural," Lambert told her.

She laughed. "I'm a whizzer on an empty street."

About the only traffic was from the carts of rocking chairs being unloaded across the street, and they pulled away one at a time as Mr. Spake's collectors emptied them.

"You'll get used to traffic," Lambert told her. "Ride again this evening. There's never much on Sundays."

He thought about using a riding lesson as an excuse not to hunt spiderwebs with Frances and decided his mother wouldn't accept it. Besides, all Miss Beeman needed was to get used to traffic—little by little, no matter what bossy Frances said. He gave Miss Beeman another pep talk and wheeled the bicycle back to the basement.

Each time he went in or out, he sneaked a look at the house next door. When they left for church, Lambert was almost sure one of the shadows in the left front window moved.

He always took a piece of string to church. Afterward, when the grown-ups gathered on the walk or under the trees, Lambert found a stick and practiced tying knots. As long as he was busy and kept his back turned, people seemed to think he didn't hear. It was a perfect way to detect, but he half-filled a stick with triple lark-heads before he heard anything besides how hot it was. Then it was Mrs. Van Horne saying it wasn't the heat she minded but the lack of festivity in New York in summer.

"Give a party," was Mrs. Peterson's advice.

"Mirabelle," said Mrs. Van Horne, "if there were enough interesting people in New York to attend a party, I wouldn't be going to Saratoga. Ah, there's my carriage."

Lambert handed her into it. She'd said yesterday that she was going "a little early" to an engagement. But Lambert had learned from Molly that soon after they'd left for the cable car, Mrs. Van Horne had come home in a hansom cab. He guessed this Sunday dinner at her brother's had been the engagement she meant. All that bother to support Miss Beeman, to put a little steel in her spine. Lambert wished she could do as much for him.

Maybe something showed. As she put up her parasol, Mrs. Van Horne smiled down at him and said, "Don't let

Frances bully you. She takes after her grandfather, and old Samuel was a tartar."

"Thank you," said Lambert, which Mrs. Van Horne didn't seem to think a strange answer. She winked as she drove away.

The talk among the men was now about gambling parlors.

"Peculiar thing," said a portly man with a heavy gold watch chain. "The police know all the likely places for them to show up, but once they're closed down, lately, they vanish."

"Finally stamping them out," was one man's guess, but even he didn't sound as if he believed it.

"Found a clever new place," said another.

"Gone to Saratoga for the season, like everybody else." Which brought a laugh.

"It's a moot question now, anyway," said the portly man. "The police are too busy saving Mr. Spake's collectors to do anything else."

That started the men guessing how much Mr. Spake was making on his chairs. About three hundred dollars a day, one man figured.

"When they're all in place," he added.

"If they ever all get in place," said another voice.

Which turned the talk to how the heat would affect the troubles in the park. As usual, just when things were getting interesting, Mrs. Grew decided it was time to go home.

The help had Sunday off after breakfast, so Sunday dinner (the only noon meal Mrs. Grew provided her guests) was always a cold buffet. Because Miss Beeman was the only one home, she told Mrs. Grew, "Please don't set the dining room just for me. We can eat in the kitchen."

"It's cooler there, too," said Lambert. And his mother would let him take off his jacket.

Mrs. Grew let herself be persuaded. Miss Beeman helped and it was almost like family. The ladies even began trading stories of their escapades as young girls. None of them came up to what Frances was planning for tonight.

He was in his room, wondering what to put in his father's carpetbag, when his mother called him to the telephone. Lambert hated talking on the telephone. He had to stand on a footstool to reach the mouthpiece. It made him feel like a baby.

Frances wasn't that much taller. She had to be standing on something, too, but it didn't seem to bother her. She was as bossy as ever.

"Bring *two* pairs of old pants for tonight," she told him. "I can't crawl in tunnels with these skirts."

"What tunnels? Listen, we're not . . . . "

"Someone's coming." There was a click, then only the hum and crackle of the wire.

At least he knew what to pack now. He put in a pair of suspenders, too, pleased there was something Frances didn't know.

He still had hours to wait. He opened the *Police Gazette* to the Pinkerton story but only read one column.

He found a lined pad and a pencil stub and wrote a report on the house next door, from the first time he saw the gas men to the movement he might have seen in the window. Then he read it over, pretending he was Mr. Pinkerton reviewing a new case. And Mr. Pinkerton could find no evidence of felonies or malefactions.

The men had gone into the house three days and possibly two nights. But somebody might have bought the house and wanted changes made quickly. The men didn't have to be from the gas company. Lambert had just guessed they were the first time he saw them and had gone on thinking of them as gas men. They could be doing all kinds of remodeling inside.

Digging a new cellar?

But there was nothing in the report to show that the workmen had put the dirt in the backyard. The new owners might have had it spread there for some reason. Lambert couldn't think what it could be, but a Pinkerton had to investigate every possibility. And besides, Mrs. Van Horne was right; Lambert shouldn't let Frances boss him around.

He'd do some bossing for a change. He'd make her telephone Beth Ann and ask if the house had new owners.

Frances agreed so quickly that Lambert felt cheated. He couldn't hear Beth Ann, but it was easy to figure what she said from listening to Frances. By the time Frances hung up, Lambert felt sorry for her. She hadn't heard from Beth Ann since she'd moved, and all Beth Ann had wanted to talk about was her new dog and horse and all the trips she'd been taking in the new carriage.

"She doesn't even miss me," wailed Frances. "And we were *best friends*!"

She looked ready to cry. Lambert wished he were someplace else. He watched Frances kick her footstool to the front door and back, then asked whether the corner house had been sold.

Frances put her nose in the air and mimicked Beth Ann. "'Of course not, Frances. *Nobody* wants to live down *there* anymore.'"

Then the men weren't from the gas company or the new electric company or remodeling the house. Lambert didn't think they were digging for treasure, either, but they were up to something they shouldn't be.

The butler came to ask if they were ready for supper. They ate from silver trays in the library. The room was two stories high with a balcony and sliding ladders on each level so people could reach the books. The food, though, didn't stand up to Mrs. Magee's. Frances said it was better when her uncle was home. After that, all she talked about was their coming expedition.

"When we detect something nefarious," she said, "Beth Ann's father will be grateful."

Lambert figured that meant it would show Beth Ann something or other. But the lady who'd lost her dog had been grateful, and catching malefactors should be worth more than a quarter.

"And when we find the treasure," she went on, "we'll be written up in the *Post* and the *Herald*. Maybe even the *Times*."

And the *Police Gazette* might pay Lambert for his own

personal account of the capture of the felons. He could put in a fight before he and Frances escaped out the gate this morning and change the movement he thought he'd seen at the window to a man with a gun, waiting to ambush him.

He wished he hadn't thought that. An ambush seemed all too likely. Maybe those men were just waiting for snoopers tonight. But Frances said she knew a secret way into Beth Ann's old yard, and, what was more important, she'd been calling him Spike all day and he was afraid he'd be Lambie again if he didn't go.

They played Halma, jumping colored marbles across a star-shaped board. They were tied at five games each when it was time to leave. Frances had told Mrs. Ridge that night spiders didn't spin their webs until after nine o'clock. By the time they had changed to Lambert's old knee pants (Frances wore hers under her skirt), collected Frances's basket and answered Mrs. Ridge's questions about how long they'd be and whether night spiders were poisonous, it was closer to ten o'clock than nine.

Mr. Ward's garden smelled like the florist's on Sixth Avenue, the one with the pool and blooming shrubs. The statues Lambert had seen from his window were mostly naked. He wished there were a full moon so he could get a better look. But not even daylight would have helped much, the way Frances rushed him to the wall.

She stopped there to step out of her skirt, wad it up and shove it in the basket. She left the basket under a tree, climbed up and crawled out on a branch until it bent enough to touch the wall. When she moved onto the wall, the branch snapped up. Before it stopped swaying, Lambert's weight was forcing it back down.

He wasn't going to give her a chance to call, "Come on, Lambie," the way she had in the park. He hung full length from the wall and it wasn't much of a drop.

They were in a lane older than any of the houses on Washington Square. It jogged around property, between walls and board fences, and ended at the gate to the drying yard of Beth Ann's old house. The gate was sure to be padlocked.

"Even if it wasn't," Frances whispered, "we couldn't use it. It makes a noise you can hear inside."

Lambert thought again of an ambush.

Frances counted boards, knelt and tugged at the bottom of one. It came free. So did the one next to it. They'd been held by single small nails. All these years she'd been playing with Beth Ann, Lambert had never suspected them of sneaking in and out at night.

"How often did you use this?" he whispered.

"Never. Beth Ann's a scaredy-cat." Frances held the board ends apart and jerked her head at the opening.

Lambert wondered what had happened to "ladies first." But a Spike couldn't be a scaredy-cat. He climbed into the deep shadow of the drying yard, turning sideways to get his shoulders through the triangular opening.

It was an even tighter fit for Frances. She stuck halfway and Lambert hoped she'd back out. But she pushed into the yard and stood up. The shadows were so deep Lambert could hardly see her.

They crept along the fence so they wouldn't walk into

the clothes poles or the wire lines. There was cheering across the street. Lambert bumped into Frances.

"Here." She found his hand and put it on what felt like a flour sack. Except nobody would store flour outside, and it was too firm and lumpy. Lambert felt one of the bigger lumps. A stone. Dirt! Bags of dirt were stacked along the fence, high as Lambert's head. He began to believe in the tunnel.

CHAPTER
TEN

They crouched against the board fence and peeked carefully around the edge of the opening, one pair of eyes above the other. Street light reflected down the passage and filtered through the trees on the Fifth Avenue side. It made the planted yard just enough lighter than the drying yard to show it was empty—unless somebody was hiding under a bush. The house was completely dark.

Frances whispered, "They must have left."

"Or they have the windows covered," said Lambert.

The chanting from the park was louder. They could make out the words: "We pay no more! We pay no more! We pay no more for Clauson and Spake!"

"They sound mad," Lambert said. The crowd in Madison Square had seemed like the ones that gathered around street fights. But the men across the street sounded as if they wanted to do the fighting themselves. He told Frances, "Mr. Spake put his rocking chairs in the park today."

"I know. Mrs. Ridge and I walked home through the

park this afternoon. Mr. Spake didn't leave one single bench."

No wonder the men were mad. Their families probably lived in hot, crowded rooms south of the square. They needed the relief of the park most and couldn't afford to pay for a chair. They were adding another verse to their chant, but it was drowned by the rattling of police clackers in all directions. One sounded almost in front of the house.

Suddenly light shone on the grass, quickly blocked by two men hurrying from the rear basement door. Frances felt down Lambert's arm and took his hand.

". . . those chairs again," the second man was saying. "Didn't you hear about Sandor the Great raising a smoke about 'em last night up in Madison Square? Well, this here's more of the same thing."

The man in the lead paused. "You think Sandor the Great's over there now?"

"Well, I think we should have a look-see." They could hear the grin in his voice. "Just to be sure it ain't got nothin' to do with us."

"Just from in front of the house."

"Aw, Mel . . . . "

Still arguing, the men moved into the passage between the houses. Frances gripped Lambert's hand hard.

Lambert patted it with his free one, giving comfort as a gentleman should. Soon as the men were back in the house, he'd lead Frances back to the loose boards and safety. He was feeling like Dick O'Dare in *The Rescue at Sea* when Frances yanked on his hand and pulled him off balance. When he got it back, he was halfway to the open

85

basement door. Frances gave another yank and then shushed him for stumbling down the basement steps.

Lambert opened his mouth, then shut it. They were already in the house, and arguing was more dangerous than going along. Those men might be on their way back right now. At least Frances knew the house well enough to get them to the front door in the dark.

The only light came from coal-oil railroad lanterns. Either Beth Ann's father had had the gas turned off or the men didn't want the meter to show they were in the house. The lanterns led like bread crumbs down the basement hall and through the kitchen to a hole broken in the wall next to the stove. Picks, shovels and six more lanterns waited beside the hole, which led to a freshly dug tunnel. Far down it shone a single lantern.

Frances turned and grinned at him. Lambert braced himself for her I-told-you-so-Lambie. She said, "Better bring one of those lanterns, Spike."

He swallowed his suggestion that she lead them to the front door. Instead, he nodded at the lantern in the tunnel and said, "We'll take that one." A Spike wouldn't let her boss him around. Besides, they didn't have time to look for matches.

He led the way into the tunnel so he could set the pace. With a little luck, they could take a look at what the men were doing and be upstairs when they came back. But before they reached the lantern, Lambert could see another glowing even farther away.

He couldn't hurry any faster. The tunnel was roughly dug and so small that even he had to bow his head. The men must have to walk doubled over. They couldn't be planning to use it much.

Frances, stumbling behind him, had the same thought. "Soon as they get the treasure out," she told him, "they'll put the dirt bags in here, patch the kitchen wall and nobody will know they've been here."

"Except us." She'd been right about the tunnel; why not the treasure, too? Lambert would get a crack machine like Mr. Carter's, and it wouldn't matter if he grew out of it. He'd just buy a bigger one. Or maybe he'd just get a carriage and coachman like Mrs. Van Horne.

The tunnel ended at the second lantern and another jagged hole. Lambert picked up the lantern, held it through the hole and leaned in after it.

The men had broken into the side of a much larger tunnel, its blue tile walls clean enough to reflect the light. Lambert closed his eyes and figured the turns they'd made since entering the house. It was the right direction.

Frances poked him. "What is it? What did they find?"

Lambert moved into the larger tunnel so she could see for herself. She stepped in after him and turned completely around, inspecting the blue walls curving over them. The tunnel was round except for a flat space at the bottom, wide enough for a pair of rails leading north and south into darkness.

"Mr. Beach's subway," Lambert told her. "We're under Fifth Avenue."

So much for Captain Kidd's treasure and his crack Columbia. He didn't object when Frances took the lantern from him, only when she started walking south between the rails. "Hey!" The walls threw the word back at him. He glanced at the tunnel they'd left and jogged half a dozen steps to catch up with Frances.

"Those men ..." he whispered.

"... have dug another tunnel from Mr. Beach's subway to the treasure under the park," Frances finished for him. "Why dig all the way under the street when somebody's already made a tunnel you can use?"

Lambert agreed that the men had used the empty house to locate Mr. Beach's subway, but he didn't think they'd find another newly dug tunnel. Whatever the men wanted with the subway, it wasn't to dig treasure from under the park. When they dug from Mr. Beach's tunnel, how could they be sure they'd hit the treasure chest first try? Or even the second or third? It was just too much work for something that might not be there. He didn't say anything to Frances, though. She was headed in the right direction, even if for the wrong reason.

Mrs. Van Horne had mentioned a Washington Square station. Since it wasn't where they'd come in, it must be on the other side of the square. Even if the men discovered the missing lantern, they wouldn't be trapped in the tunnel. If their head start was long enough.

Lambert took out his knife and walked backward, guarding their rear. He'd have to get so close to use the knife that the men could hold him at arm's length. They'd probably laugh at him. But the little penknife was all he had. And it made him feel better.

"Look at this!" said Frances.

"Shhhh!" Lambert told her. Then he turned and said, "Holy gee!" just as loudly.

It was round and fit the tunnel like a plug. But there was a door, and oval windows on each side of it reflected the lantern's light. The door stood open. They climbed the metal steps to the little platform and stepped inside. Coal-oil lamps and vases for flowers still stood on the tables that were set midway in the two rows of red plush seats. When Frances held up the lantern, they could see the upholstery was rotting and the lamp bases tarnished.

Frances pushed a vase. It wasn't fastened to the table. Neither was the lamp.

"It really must have been a smooth ride," she said.

Lambert nodded. There was no doubt it was Mr. Beach's subway car.

"It's a lot nicer than the horsecars. Cleaner, too. Even after all these years. Maybe if someone took . . . ."

Lambert grabbed her arm and she hushed. He peered out the back of the car but could see nothing beyond the door. But the sound he'd heard was closer. He shoved Frances toward the door at the other end of the car. *"Run!"*

She did. But only until she spotted the bags piled on the end of the seat row. They looked like the money bags in cartoons but without dollar signs painted on them.

"Too heavy," Lambert told her, and shoved her again. "Get the door open."

Since he had to wait and the penknife was in his hand, Lambert slit one of the bags. Blue disks slid out. Lambert had never seen any before but he knew what they were. He shoved a handful in his pocket just as Frances left the platform and took most of the light with her. Lambert stumbled after her. The men following had been left with even less light. As Lambert jumped down to the tracks, the car shook and a man yelped. They were closer than Lambert had guessed.

He ran after Frances and wondered if he should tell her to douse the lantern. It made it too easy for the men chasing them. But it would be harder for Lambert and Frances to run in the dark, and they might need the lantern at the station. If the station was still there.

Frances had tucked her hair under a boy's cap. It had a big shiny button sewn in the center. Lambert kept his eye on the button and ran. His legs got heavier at every step and he panted so hard he couldn't hear the men chasing them. But he kept up with the button and slammed into Frances before he realized she'd stopped at a door.

It looked new and the hinges made no sound when Frances opened it. Lambert shut the men in the dark and looked for a key. There wasn't any. A lot of tables were stored in the cellar, each covered with a canvas dust sheet. Lambert started pushing one against the door. It was heavier than any table he knew. Frances set down the lantern and helped. Hands patted the other side of the door, feeling for the knob.

Steep plank stairs were the only other exit. The lantern flickered out before they reached them. Lambert grabbed Frances's sleeve with one hand and flailed out with the other. If he hadn't been looking at the stair railing when the lantern died, he'd never have found it. One of the men rammed his shoulder into the door. The table moved. The "bump-scritch" followed them up the steps.

The door at the top was closed but light shone under it. "Bang-scritch" went the table and door, and the men grunted as they squeezed through. Circling the table in the dark would confuse them. They'd have trouble finding the stairs until Lambert opened the door. Already he could hear them bumping and cussing. The ear he put to the door heard other men's voices.

Lambert tugged Frances up beside him and whispered, "Card players, I think.... We go straight through ... no stopping ... on the word."

The fumbling men didn't seem to be any closer to the stairs, so he took a precious minute to get some of his breath back.

"One!" he whispered to Frances. "Two!"

"Here!" said a man from bottom of the stairs.

"GO!" yelled Lambert, and threw open the door.

CHAPTER ELEVEN

They burst into a small room made even smaller by walls of wooden packing cases. Some had been restacked to make a poker table. Four men looked up from their cards, open mouthed, as Lambert charged past.

"Hey!" One started up, bumped the table crates and scattered red, white and blue chips. Lambert skidded on them and stumbled head first through a curtained doorway he hoped led to a shop.

It did. And there was nothing blocking the doorway on the other side. The proprietor was as surprised as the poker players. Lambert righted himself and ran around a dusty counter to the street door. When he opened the door, a bell over it jangled and someone in the back room yelled, "Get 'em!" It sounded like Mel from the tunnel.

Frances had kept close behind, but the tobacco shop man was over his surprise. He lunged for her, arms out. Frances tipped a cigar case over in front of him and leaped for the door. Lambert held it open until she was through. Ladies first.

The sidewalk was crowded with people hoping for cooler air. As Lambert dodged and skipped around them, he kept glancing back. Six men came out of the tobacco shop and after them. The proprietor was too old for a chase. And Lambert and Frances were too tired.

They gained a little at the corner. A hurdy-gurdy man had collected a crowd under the arc light. People at the edges grinned and made way for Lambert and Frances, but the men, Lambert noticed when he glanced back, were having trouble getting through.

They were on Washington Square but the wrong side. Home was across the park, a long run. Even longer if they didn't go through the park. But there'd be dark, lonely places in the park. Lambert didn't want the men to catch them there. Their only hope was staying with the crowd. When they crossed the street, they had to dodge carts and carriages and nervous horses. Somehow Frances came out in the lead. And she ran straight into the park.

Lambert didn't have breath to call her back. He hardly had enough to keep going. The heat was wearing him out faster than the running. And there wasn't anyone, *anyone!* Where were all the policemen who'd been rattling for help when Frances pulled him into the empty house? And where were the ones who must have answered?

On the other side, Lambert thought grimly. Where the trouble was. Where the . . . . He'd been too busy breathing and running to pay attention to other things. He tried to hear above his heart thumps and gaspy breaths. The closest sound was that of the men chasing them. It put a fraction more speed into his legs, but he still wouldn't have caught up to Frances if she hadn't stumbled.

He didn't waste air on words. He grunted and shouldered her onto a cross path that led toward shouting. When they reached it, Lambert could hardly lift his feet, and the men were only half a dozen yards behind them.

About twenty men were arguing with four of Mr. Spake's collectors. Not a single policeman. But as he staggered up, Lambert heard enough to know why the rows of rocking chairs were empty: The collectors were tossing out nonpaying sitters. Lambert pushed through the angry group, spotted the chairs he wanted and dropped into one. Frances plunked down next to him.

Between pants she told him, "Long as we're . . . not paying . . . you should've picked . . . ones with arms."

Lambert didn't have breath to explain why he hadn't. He barely managed to change a couple of his painful gasps to, "Hang on . . . no matter what." He gripped the side edges of the chair seat.

Gray trousers stopped in front of them. "That'll be three cents each."

Lambert kept his head down. A sideways glance showed Mel's friends stopping a few feet away. Two of the men still had their playing cards.

"Okay, you kids," said a familiar voice. "Get off them chairs."

A second pair of gray trousers joined the first. A hard-toed shoe reached out and tramped on the rocker of Lambert's chair. The chair jerked forward. At the same time, Biff Finnegan pulled on Lambert's arm. Lambert hung onto the seat.

One of the men who'd been arguing with the collectors yelled, "Leave the kids alone!"

"Pick on somebody your own size," yelled another.

Biff let go of Lambert's arm. He grabbed the top of the chair back, pulled it forward and tried to shake Lambert off. Lambert hooked his feet around the chair legs and hung on, staring down at the hard-toed boots.

"Hey! Quit that!"

"Save the kids!"

The group of angry men charged the collectors. But the men from the tobacco shop reached Lambert and Frances first. Two of them grabbed the backs of their chairs and started pulling them away backward. The angry crowd mistook them for un-uniformed collectors and started fighting them, too. Lambert could only tell friend from felon by the direction his chair was being dragged. He worried that the chairs would be pulled apart and he and Frances trampled under the fighters.

Then clackers rattled and Lambert glimpsed the high domes of police helmets. The heck with Spike LeGrew. Lambert yelled for help at the top of his lungs. Frances was screeching even louder.

His chair stopped and rocked violently as it was let go. Then it was caught and raised from the ground until he was looking down at the fighting. Lambert clung to the chair as it jerked and settled. He risked a sideways look.

Frances's chair was even with his. Her cap had come off and her hair hung loose.

"Look, it's a girl!" people were crying.

Lambert looked down between the chairs at the grinning face from Miss Beeman's poster. Sandor was doing his encore, balancing their chairs on his shoulders, holding onto the outside rungs.

Had he been skulking around the park just waiting for a chance to perform? He'd have to give *that* picture of Sandor to Miss Beeman. Only it didn't seem fair when Sandor had just rescued them from the tobacco-store felons. Besides, Miss Beeman had gotten angry when Mrs. Van Horne had suggested his manager might plan something like this. Lambert supposed he should be grateful. He just wished Frances would stop grinning and waving to people.

A stout little man he guessed was Sandor's manager bustled up with two men who were already sketching Sandor holding the chairs.

Bossy Frances pointed and said, "Can we go that way, please?"

The stout man walked backward in front of Sandor and asked, "What's that way?"

"Home," said Frances, and gave him Lambert's address.

"Can you make it?" the man asked Sandor.

"Easy, Mr. Wilkes," said Sandor.

Mr. Wilkes trotted away. A newspaperman took his place and called questions to Sandor.

Lambert wished he wouldn't. When Sandor talked, the chair made alarming sideslips. It was frightening enough when he just walked. Then one of the newspaper artists recognized Frances, and word that she was Mr. Ward's niece brought more reporters, all shouting questions and trying to get close. Lambert hung on, his mouth dry, picturing what would happen if they tripped Sandor. Before they did, Mr. Wilkes came back, beaming, and led Sandor out of the park to where police were holding up traffic so he could cross the street to Lambert's house.

His mother and Mrs. Van Horne were watching from the stoop. Mrs. Van Horne smiled hugely when she saw them. When Mrs. Grew recognized who was in the chairs, she gave a cry and came to meet them. But Sandor carried them past her, clear up to the stoop, where he turned around to face the followers while Mr. Wilkes helped lower the chairs. The crowd whistled and cheered and called for a speech.

From the way Frances was grinning and waving, she'd have been happy to oblige. Lambert edged up behind her and whispered, "Those men are probably in that crowd and now they know where we live."

She started to pull down her hand, then stopped and went on waving. Still smiling, she turned her head just enough to whisper, "We've got to tell somebody. Somebody who'll make the police act fast."

Her uncle could have done it, only he wasn't around. That left Mrs. Van Horne. Before Lambert could reach her, Mr. Wilkes stepped up to the ladies and said, "I'm

97

sorry, ma'am, but this crowd won't let us leave. If we could just step inside for a while . . . ."

Sandor was taking a speech-making pose, holding his arms up for silence. Mr. Wilkes hauled on his jacket, muttered, "Not now," and somehow herded everyone into the hall and shut the front door.

Lambert's mother looked as if someone had raised an improper subject at dinner. Not only hadn't she been introduced to Sandor and Mr. Wilkes, she wouldn't have invited them to visit if she had. But here they were. And Sandor, at least, had rescued Lambert and Frances from something. Everyone watched her, waiting. She smiled and led the way into the parlor.

Mrs. Van Horne looked as pleased as Mr. Wilkes. Lambert was sorry he had to make her miss what happened next. But while he was searching for something to use as a signal, Frances stepped up and said, "May I speak to you privately, Mrs. Van Horne? It's very personal."

Mrs. Van Horne excused herself to the men who were waiting for her to enter the parlor first. Then she stepped across the hall and opened the door to her own parlor. When Lambert tried to follow Frances in, Mrs. Van Horne said, "Not you, Lambert," and closed the door firmly in his face. But he'd hardly started his short list of cuss words when the door opened again.

"Sorry," Mrs. Van Horne told him. The corners of her lips twitched. "It isn't as personal as I thought."

Lambert glared at Frances and she didn't interrupt his short account of the tunnel and the chase. Then they followed Mrs. Van Horne back across the hall to the telephone.

"Hello, Central," she said. "Connect me with the police commissioner wherever he may be. . . . Aren't there telephones on Coney Island? . . . Then connect me with the assistant commissioner, please. Unless he's also departed for the weekend."

During the wait for someone to answer and then summon the assistant commissioner to the telephone, there wasn't a sound from the parlor. For once Lambert's mother wasn't trying to hide her eavesdropping.

Mrs. Van Horne introduced herself in an imperial tone. "Good evening, Commissioner. This is Mrs. Van Horne. I believe you know my brother-in-law, Cornelius Van Horne. . . . Yes, very honored. I shall be sitting on the platform. Commissioner, I have learned that trespassers have taken possession of a vacant house next door and dug a tunnel into Mr. Beach's old subway. Some . . . . I don't know, Commissioner, but it must be something illegal. They chased two young friends of mine all the way to Mr. Beach's old Washington Square station where other men attempted to do them bodily harm. . . . I did not ask them, Commissioner." Her voice had become even more regal. "I do not pry into the activities of my friends. But I think you should know that one of them is Carlton Ward's niece."

She covered the mouthpiece with her hand, winked at Frances and Lambert and said, "That should get immediate action."

Mr. Wilkes, Lambert's mother and Sandor had come into the hall. Mrs. Grew's eyes were wide as she looked from Lambert to Frances and back again.

Mr. Wilkes must have noticed that Mrs. Van Horne hadn't mentioned Sandor but he didn't seem bothered. He waited while she answered the assistant commissioner's questions, gave the address of Beth Ann's old house and hung up. Then he dashed outside.

"Just to advise the police that they'll be needed next door," he said over his shoulder. But when Lambert went to shut the door, it was the newspapermen lounging on the steps he was talking to.

Mrs. Grew was leading everyone into the parlor, fanning herself hard enough to rattle her ivory fan and demanding to be told what had happened. Lambert decided to let Frances do the telling. He stepped onto the stoop and pulled the door shut behind him.

There were still a lot of people in front of the house. They pointed and gawped at him until he moved to the bench nearest the corner house. The vines screened him from the sidewalk, but when he sat in his favorite place, his back against the house, he had a clear view of Beth Ann's old front yard. He could also see Mr. Wilkes.

Mr. Wilkes waved his arms a lot. Lambert had no trouble guessing he was repeating Mrs. Van Horne's account of the tobacco-shop felons trying to do bodily harm, with a large part added about Sandor's rescue. He couldn't have told about the tunnel, though, because none of the newspapermen looked at the corner house. Lambert decided Mr. Wilkes wanted to get his story in before a new one drew the newspapermen next door.

He wondered why the police hadn't arrived. Those Mr. Wilkes had been going to advise were gone, probably back to the park. There was still a lot of yelling over there. The crowd in front of the house was blocking traffic and another battle seemed likely. Lambert looked back toward the corner and scrambled to his knees.

Bridget and Molly were walking slowly toward the house, arms linked and heads together as they wondered at all the people. Lambert waved an arm and whistled softly. Molly waved back and the two of them hurried to the basement steps where they could talk without attracting attention.

Lambert leaned down and asked if they'd seen any policemen around the corner house. They shook their heads.

"That house is empty," Molly told him.

"What's the to-do?" said Bridget.

Lambert told them, "Sandor the Great is visiting."

"*Here?*" said Molly.

"In the parlor."

"He's joshin' us," said Bridget.

"Honest." Lambert crossed his heart and held his hand up, palm out. The girls looked at each other.

"We can ask Mrs. Grew if she'll be wanting some coffee or tea," said Bridget, and they ran down to let themselves in, giggling with excitement.

Sandor would probably offer to carry the trays

... while Bridget and Molly were holding them. Lambert wondered that the commotion hadn't wakened Miss Beeman. Maybe he should knock on her door and tell her who was in the parlor. She'd probably ask to feel his biceps. Lambert was glad when Frances came out. He pulled up his legs so she'd have room to sit.

As if on her order, a paddy wagon came around the corner, followed by a carriage. They stopped in front of Beth Ann's old house. The rear doors of the wagon opened. A dozen policemen jumped out and waited for the two men in the carriage to tell them what to do.

Mr. Wilkes hurried up the steps and into the house. Everyone else rushed next door, the newspapermen drowning out each other's questions. The men from the carriage led some of the uniformed policemen through the passage to the backyard, but most were left to keep people outside the fence.

Lambert said, "Maybe you should telephone Beth Ann."

Frances snapped, "Let her read about it in the newspaper."

Lambert had been thinking of getting permission for them to go inside the fence and watch the capture but he let it go. There'd been tearfulness under the anger. He figured it was the letdown of being abandoned.

"They'll be back," he told her. "Soon as they find out who went through the tunnel."

Frances looked at him as if he were loony.

"The newspapermen." He turned to nod at them and

grabbed Frances's foot. "Look! Isn't that Miss Beeman?"

She was pushing her bicycle through the crowd. Lambert was so surprised he couldn't believe it was Miss Beeman until she was almost home. He ran to help her with the machine.

She looked as if she'd been through a battle . . . and won. She'd cycled to Madison Square, hoping to see Sandor the Great. There'd been trouble over the rocking chairs, worse than the night before. Traffic had been snarled for blocks around, but with people milling and fighting, she'd been afraid to walk the bicycle.

"I pedaled every inch of the way," she told Lambert proudly, "until I reached the corner there." She waved a handkerchief in that direction, then used it to pat her forehead. "Whatever is going on?"

"Frances will tell you. She's up on the stoop."

He forgot to warn her that Frances was wearing boys' clothes. Maybe she'd think Frances was taking up cycling. The *Police Gazette* ran pictures of young lady bicyclers wearing tight knee pants.

He had to knock twice before Bridget heard him and unlocked the basement door. She grinned at the bicycle and said, "Does she know who's upstairs?"

Lambert shoved the machine into the storeroom without answering. He was surprised to find Mr. Carter's rack still empty. Bridget told him the reason. She'd taken the telephone call from New Jersey. Most of Mr. Carter's bicycle club, including Mr. Carter, were in a hospital with heat prostration.

103

Molly came out of the kitchen with a tray of Mrs. Magee's cakes. Bridget reached for the tray, but Molly sidestepped past her toward the back stairs.

"They'll be wanting more coffee," she told Bridget. "You can take that up."

Lambert didn't need to ask why they were taking turns and ignoring the dumbwaiter. By now, Miss Beeman must know, too. He followed Molly upstairs.

Miss Beeman was perched on the edge of a parlor chair, staring at Sandor like a light-stuck rabbit. When she took her coffee from Mrs. Grew, the cup rattled on the saucer. Lambert begged two slices of sponge cake from Molly and went back to Frances.

She'd taken his seat against the wall, her arms around her pulled-up legs. She could never sit like that in a skirt—which reminded him that Frances's was back in her uncle's garden. He handed her a slice of cake and jerked his head at the crowd in front of the corner house. It had grown a lot.

"Think you can get past them if I lend you another cap?" he said.

Frances laid the slice of cake on her knees and broke off a piece. "I'm not going home," she told him. "Your mother telephoned Mrs. Ridge and asked if I could stay here overnight."

Lambert sat sideways on the bench. "Did she say why?"

"Unforeseen circumstances." Frances smiled at the bit of cake between her fingers. "Mrs. Ridge still thinks we're hunting night spiders."

"How will you get your skirt?" Lambert had already decided to say yes when she asked him to crawl back through the fence and climb her uncle's wall. It was the sort of thing Gentleman Spike LeGrew would do. Besides, he was acquiring a taste for undercover work.

But Frances said, "I'll telephone Roger tomorrow morning."

"Roger?"

"The butler. He's used to getting Uncle Carlton out of scrapes. He won't mind getting my skirt for me."

She still hadn't eaten a bite of cake. Lambert had finished his. He said, "If you don't want that, I'll eat it."

She handed the slice of cake over without a word. Lambert figured she was worried about her own scrape and what her uncle was going to do about it. If he locked her in the house for the summer, at least she wouldn't have to collect any more spiderwebs. Before he could pass on that bit of comfort, the two police officials from the carriage strode through the gate next door and led the newspapermen and half the crowd toward the Grew house.

"It's about time," said Lambert, and gulped down the cake so he'd be ready to shake hands.

CHAPTER
TWELVE

The police officials came up to the stoop and banged the door knocker. While they waited for Bridget to open the door, they noticed Lambert and Frances on the bench. But they removed their hats and stepped inside without even a nod. Lambert and Frances stared at each other.

"They can't know," said Lambert. "Who we are, I mean." He tried to sound surer than he felt.

Bridget opened the door and waved them inside. Lambert stood up and grinned and made a bow, gesturing with his arm for Frances to go first. She swept past like Mrs. Astor. But after they told their stories, they were sent back out, as if they'd had no part in what had happened. It was grown-up business now.

At least the newspapermen appreciated them. They listened to their stories, asked a million questions and had them pose together and separately for the artists. But Lambert made sure that either he or Frances stayed on the bench in front of the parlor window to eavesdrop until they found out what had happened.

Now the stout man from church would learn where the gambling parlors had gone. Somebody had remembered Mr. Beach's old subway but nobody knew if any of the stations were left. Lambert had been right: They'd used the corner house just to break into the subway so they could find a station. Another day or two and the tunnel would have been gone, refilled with the dirt bags and the wall patched. And gambling parlors would be set up in the tunnel on each side of the three stations still left.

The newspapermen left with the police officials, but the crowd grew, blocking traffic. Everyone in New York seemed to be coming to gawk at the two houses. From time to time they started a chant for Sandor. They even tried to steal the two rocking chairs he'd carried. Lambert and Frances moved them into the hall.

Lambert wondered if his mother would let him charge people to see the chairs: a penny a look, three cents to sit. After all, she was letting Sandor and Mr. Wilkes stay overnight.

Lambert and Frances had moved to the bench with the shield of vines, the one next to Mrs. Van Horne's parlor window. When she brought Lambert's mother into her parlor for advice, Lambert and Frances couldn't help overhearing them.

Mr. Wilkes had been hinting for an invitation, saying it was dangerous for Sandor to leave with the crowd getting bigger.

"Nonsense," was Mrs. Van Horne's opinion. "It's just a way to keep Sandor's name in the newspapers another day. He'll have all the newspapermen back when Sandor leaves tomorrow."

"But . . ."—Mrs. Grew's ivory fan rattled—"but what will people think?"

"That they'd like to sleep where Sandor did. Put him in the suite and Mr. Wilkes in the vacant room. Invite them as guests. I guarantee you'll have people lining up to rent that suite. The room, too, no doubt."

Frances had her feet on the bench, her arms wrapped around them. She rested her chin on her knees and asked Lambert, "Do you ever get mysterious guests?"

"What?" Lambert had been watching a man drop a cigar butt on the steps, and worrying about the morning. Even if Mrs. Van Horne was right, they wouldn't have a third maid tomorrow and the sidewalk looked like Fifth Avenue after a torchlight parade.

"Mysterious guests," Frances repeated, "with huge locked trunks, or get cryptic messages left by mysterious strangers."

Lambert thought of a couple of messages left by Mrs. Van Horne's different clubs. And her boxes and trunks in the basement. If Frances found out about those, it would be worse than Captain Kidd's treasure.

"Detectives are supposed to detect," she was saying, just as if he were a little kid. Then she added, "We need another case, Spike."

But it wasn't going to work. She wasn't going to bully and trick him again. He told her, "Don't forget the reports. You still have to write those. And what about your uncle? He's coming home tomorrow. What'll he say when he sees the newspapers?"

"That I'm industrious, resourceful and an A-One shaker and mover."

Lambert had to grin. "Double-A-One," he added.

It was true. Besides, Mr. Ward probably wouldn't let her out of the house until fall. Maybe he'd even hire a tutor for her, the way his father had. Lambert rested his head on his knees, suddenly very tired.

The chase, he decided, and the letdown after all the excitement. He didn't hang back when his mother called them in to bed. Though he did wave when some of the crowd gave them a ragged cheer as they crossed the stoop.

When he undressed for bed, he found four blue gambling chips in his pocket, all that were left of the handful he'd taken from Mr. Beach's subway car. He set two aside to give Frances in the morning.

But when he woke, it was nearly noon. The sweeping had been done (Mr. Wilkes had paid the street cleaner to sweep in front of both houses), and a huge thank-you bouquet had arrived for his mother. Bridget was mad at Molly for not sharing the two dollars she'd gotten for telling a newspaperman what Sandor had eaten for breakfast. Mrs. Magee was banging pots and yelling at everyone because they'd let her sleep through the whole thing. And Frances, as well as Sandor and his manager, was gone.

She didn't telephone, either, though almost everybody else in New York did. He decided to walk up Fifth Avenue

109

and meet Miss Beeman after work. Since he was going to pass the Ward house, he could stop and get his carpetbag. But before six o'clock, the gardener brought it back. He also delivered thank-you notes for Lambert's mother—one from Frances and one from her uncle—and a note, sealed with gobs of green wax, for Lambert.

Lambert's read: "Taking night boat to Providence for Fourth of July. Return Saturday. Be alert for Mysterious Guest. Signed, F. Ward, AA-1 Detective."

Bossy Frances, acting as if being detectives had been her idea. He hoped she'd stay in Providence.

The Fourth of July was the hottest day so far. Mrs. Van Horne's brother-in-law cut his speech short.

"Because of the heat, *he* says," Mrs. Van Horne told them at dinner. "But we'll see what the newspapers say tomorrow." She'd worn a sash across her bosom printed with LET ME VOTE, TOO.

She was worn from the heat, though, and didn't go up to the roof to watch the fireworks at the Battery. As usual, the fireworks brought rain. Storm after storm swept the city through the next day. Lambert thought of the Providence boat but decided Frances would never get seasick. He was right.

Early Saturday, while he was trying to keep a sidewalk full of trunks from getting mixed, nosy Frances came with her basket.

"You moving, Spike?" she said.

"No, but everybody else is." Mrs. Van Horne's trunks had rounded tops, so railroad men had to load them right

110

side up. They weren't very good for sitting, either. Lambert propped himself against one and crossed his ankles. "These are being picked up for shipping to Saratoga and those are going to the second-floor suite."

Frances rested her basket on the trunk top next to Lambert. "Who'd you get?" she whispered.

"A writer."

"Maybe he's a Bohemian, one of those freethinkers from the other side of the park. A lot of them are anarchists."

"This writer," he said, "is fifty-two and his books are so highbrow nobody understands them. Excuse me."

He jumped up to check the label on the trunk two porters were taking into the house. It didn't belong to the new guest. The men traded it for another. Lambert checked that label, too.

When he got back to Frances, she was holding two brown leather notebooks. Both had AA-1 DETECTIVES printed in gold on the cover. In the corner of one were Frances's initials; on the other, "S. LeG."

Lambert blinked and ran his fingers over the gold letters. Spike LeGrew. Detective Spike LeGrew. The letters made it real. It wasn't until she finished telling how she'd ordered them in Providence that he realized sneaky Frances had made them partners.

He dug in his pocket for the two blue chips he'd been carrying every day. "Here." He put them in her hand. "Your share of the treasure."

For once he'd surprised her. She looked up. "How did you get them?"

He propped himself against the trunk, folded his arms and told her. "Oh," he added, "and Beth Ann's father came yesterday and told me he was grateful."

Frances stared at him. "*Told* you? No reward?"

Lambert shook his head. He'd do better finding lost dogs, only he'd have to find two a day, every day, to be able to buy a bicycle before school started. Frances might have an idea. Ideas were something she was good at. But he looked at the gold initials and knew that Spike LeGrew of AA-1 Detectives could never tell her about Biff Finnegan. Unless . . . .

"Frances," he said, "detectives have to follow people sometimes. We have to be fast and quick off the mark."

"Hansom cabs."

Carlton Ward's niece would think of them first. Lambert shook his head. "Not reliable. I said *quick*."

"Bicycles."

Lambert sighed and admitted, "Too expensive."

"Roller skates."

"*Roller skates?*" Lambert could see the sign: THE AA-1 FIGURE EIGHT LAMBIE DETECTIVE AGENCY. WE NEVER FALL.

"You said reliable and fast off the mark."

Then the wagon from the railroad pulled up and she started telling Lambert to check the trunks going upstairs while she watched Mrs. Van Horne's.

If Lambert knew Frances Ward, she'd take the bills of lading in to his mother and come out with an invitation to lunch. He wondered how much roller skates cost.

AUTHOR'S
NOTE

Yes, there really was a subway. But Mr. Beach dug it under Broadway, not Fifth Avenue, and it ran only a few blocks. Everything else is true, even the description of the tunnel and car as they were found by workers when the BMT subway extended its lines. The tunnel is now part of the lower level of the City Hall station in Manhattan.

Sandor is based on Sandow the Great, a handsome German strong man who dazzled New York society (especially the ladies) with his feats of strength. He endorsed Fowler bicycles and charged a hundred dollars for admission to his after-show parties, which were always crowded. But Sandow had nothing to do with the Rocking Chair Riots.

They took place in 1901, a little later than the 1890's of this story, and were in Madison Square park and Central Park. If there hadn't been a record heat wave that year, we might still be paying for chairs in our parks.

ABOUT
THE AUTHOR

BETTY BAKER's special interest in children's books began when her son, Christopher, was young, and in 1962 her first book, *Little Runner of the Longhouse,* was published for beginning readers. Since that time she has written many notable books, nonfiction as well as fiction, for young people of varying ages.

Her novels for older readers include *Seven Spells to Farewell, The Great Desert Race, Save Sirrushany!, The Spirit Is Willing* and *A Stranger and Afraid.*

She has won the Western Heritage Award for the outstanding Western juvenile book twice: for *Killer-of-Death* and *And One Was a Wooden Indian,* and her *Settlers and Strangers* was a Nonfiction Honor Book in the 1978 Boston Globe–Horn Book Awards.

Ms. Baker lives in Tucson, Arizona.